# Beyond the Mirror:

## Volume 3
## Alternate Worlds

## BLAZE WARD

Knotted Road Press
www.KnottedRoadPress.com

**Beyond the Mirror: Volume 3
Alternate Worlds**
*Copyright © 2014 Blaze Ward*
*All rights reserved.*
*Published 2014 by Knotted Road Press*
*www.KnottedRoadPress.com*

ISBN: 978-0692335833

Cover art:
Copyright © Innovari | Dreamstime.com - Earth Moon Surface Photo
Copyright © Jules315 | Dreamstime.com - Earth And Moon Photo

Cover design and interior design © 2014 Knotted Road Press
www.KnottedRoadPress.com

**Never miss a release!**

If you'd like to be notified of new releases, sign up for my newsletter.

I only send out newsletters once a quarter, will never spam you, or use your email for nefarious purposes. You can also unsubscribe at any time.

http://www.blazeward.com/newsletter/

# Beyond the Mirror:
## Volume 3
## Alternate Worlds

## Blaze Ward

# Also by Blaze Ward

### Collections
*Beyond the Mirror: Volume 1 Fantastic Worlds*
*Beyond the Mirror: Volume 2 Fantastic Worlds*

### Stories
*Approacheth the Wyvern*
*Falling into the Giant's Spine*
*Greater Than The Gods Intended*
*Lokisdotter*
*Rebels*

### Brak Stories
*The Meat Shield*
*The Popcorn Kitten*
*Destiny*

### Suren Stories
*The Slave Market*
*The Horse Thief*

### Kaleph Stories
*Death Key for the Great Khan*
*The Changestorm*

# Table of Contents

# Forward

I'm always surprised when Blaze asks me a technical question about writing. Given his skill level, I generally assume he's more experienced than he actually is.

He is an experienced storyteller. He's been telling stories all his life, practicing his craft.

These stories are evidence of that. He's finding his voice, the worlds he wants to share. The previous volumes were pure fantasy. This collection is a mixture of genres, times, and places.

I'm excited about where Blaze is going, how he's pushing boundaries to stay true to the stories he needs to tell.

I look forward to continuing these journeys with him.

I hope you're enjoying these journeys as much as I am.

Leah Cutter
December 2014

# Introduction to Volume 3

Here it is. *Beyond The Mirror, Volume 3: Alternate Worlds.* Volume three?

I look at the calendar. An entire year has passed since I sat down and said, "I can do this." And I'm still doing it.

It has been a grand adventure, accompanied by my (unindicted) co-conspirator and love of my life. I keep looking at her and saying "I could not be doing this without you." And she smiles.

So. Volume Three. Alternate Worlds.

One and Two were pure fantasy. In this volume, I wanted to branch out and do other things. As I grow in my craft, I have other stories that need telling, other places I have visited, other dreams to dream.

Speculative (read: Science) Fiction lets you go almost anywhere and explore how the worlds might be different. Here I wanted to do the same. The results were dieselpunk, time travel, lots of alternate history, literary fiction, and space opera. I like them. I hope you will as well.

I was able to enlist the assistance of several guest readers on this volume. Chuck, Elena, and Joel helped make it better than it would have been. But I want to make sure everyone knows that it wouldn't be as good as it is without the eyes of Leah (who can't spell) and Adrianne (who can). That these stories are as good as they are is a testament to having good friends. All the mistakes you find are still mine, but there are a LOT fewer of them than there would have been. Thank you.

And now, let us take a tour of several Alternate Worlds...

Blaze Ward
December, 2014

*This started off as an intended submission to an anthology where I was invited to participate. About halfway through, I realized it was the start of something much grander than I have planned (see Tatiyana, below) and that it could not wait until the middle of next year, so I kept going here and turned it into the beginning of an arc of science fiction that spans something on the order of thirty-eight centuries, which still isn't that far when you realize that it has only been about thirty-two since Menelaus set out to find his runaway bride.*

*I want to thank Chuck for making sure I got as much of the technical details right as possible. His expertise is still British Armour in the Desert campaign, but he was there when I needed an spare pair of eyes on guns, calibers, and Soviet redneck engineers. Elena was there to provide a welcome critical eye on the details of the Soviet life and how they differed from a western view. I'm probably still wrong in places, but much less wrong.*

# Valeryia
## Ambush

"Pyotr," Sergey called suddenly above the roar of the engines and the rattle of the little tank's main gun being reloaded, "stop now!"

The driver dropped the engines out of gear and pulled the steering levers to neutral in one motion, causing the heavy steel beast to shudder to a halt. He had learned not to ask why, but hung poised now over the controls, listening, anticipating. They had been a team for three years of war.

Outside, the sky abruptly lit up with howling fire and a tree next to the tank exploded from a shot that would have skewered the turret like an olive had they not stopped. Around them, the giant tank battle shrank and faded into just their tiny corner.

"Good," Sergey yelled. "Now, full speed and circle right around those trees." He felt Pyotr engage both engines and red-line them. The little British-made *Matilda* was normally a slow tank, an Infantry tank, but today she seemed to understand the urgency and jumped forward, a scrappy little Cossack pony.

Sergey poked his head out of the hatch and looked behind them. He dropped back down before more machine-gun fire erupted. "Slava, set the turret to five o'clock, depress five degrees, and go for a track shot. We're bow-on with a type IV panzer. You'll be lined up when Pyotr turns."

The gunner nodded and began to spin the turret, watching Sergey instead of the gunsight until a hand sign stopped him. He put an eye to the lens and found the trigger. "Ready."

Simultaneously, the little tank completed her turn and raced for cover.

Slava waited.

Sergey tapped him on the shoulder, blind inside the armor. "Now."

Slava pulled the trigger, willing to trust the Lieutenant's instincts. As the gun went off, the Panzer came into the crosshairs. Slava watched the shot slam into the panzer's right side tracks and blow them off the wheel.

Above, Sergey popped open the hatch and fired a smoke grenade at the German beast to cover their escape.

Behind them, tanks and men died.

# The Arrival

Sergey looked up from his book and considered the falling snow. It fell in big, fluffy, flat, cotton balls, laden with moisture, there was so little wind tonight. More than a foot of snow had already accumulated while they waited in this little stand of trees, hidden from the German Panzers that had been hunting them earlier. It insulated the tent he sat in while he read, kept him warm enough that he could stay out of the tank's turret while his crew worked.

But now, he was out of hot water for his tea. Sergey stood, adjusted his padded skullcap and long coat, and tucked his dog-earred copy of *The Iliad* back into his pocket. After three years at war, it was his most prized possession, a lone connection to the promises of his youth and a life of intellectual contemplation amidst the scholars of Moscow and Leningrad. He sighed. Perhaps, he would return. After the war.

Before Sergey left the warmth of his little tent, he poked his head out and scanned the sky. There had been few breaks in the clouds for four days now. Last night, an aurora had turned the sky a swirling pastel of reds and blues, unlike he or his crewmates had ever seen. Perhaps it had finally passed and the radio would work again. And the compass. The maps he had been given couldn't show them where they were either as they were crude and most-likely wrong. Or the tank had simply gone off the map's western edge. Again. The Nazis were running out of places to hide.

Sergey emerged into a stillness almost deathly and trudged across the three meters of space to the bow of his tank. As always, he reverently touched the black letters elegantly painted on the white-washed green paint.

*Валерия.*

Valeriya.

A pretty, blond girl with bright, blue eyes. She haunted Sergey's dreams, sitting in a Moscow park he had never visited. He knew he would find her there. After the war. Until then, his chariot bore her name.

He grabbed a handhold and mounted the bow and tread deck to reach the turret. The British called the vehicle an Infantry Tank, Mark II, commonly, a *Matilda*. It had been Sergey and his crew's home for three years now, even with a month off to remove the little British pop-gun from the turret and replace it with a much-larger *ZiS-5* cannon from a dead comrade. And to weld a mount for the big *DShk* machine gun Sergey could fire if he felt like being out in the fury of battle. The machine gun was almost a security blanket, some days.

Sergey stuck his head into an open hatch and looked down at his gunner. "Is the radio working yet, Senior Slava?" He could not help the nickname. Two crewmen named Vyacheslav, out of four, both of them old enough to be his father. It was even funnier calling the younger of the two "Junior Slava." They were all family now. Junior Slava had a daughter he threatened to introduce Sergey to, a fat little Komi girl.

After the war.

The balding man looked up with an exasperated sigh, one headphone off and one listening. "No, Sergey," he said. "All frequencies are static, some of it so dense that it sounds like music." He looked down and fiddled with dials, cursing under his breath.

Sergey shrugged and looked at *Valeriya's* rear deck. Pyotr, the baby of the crew at nineteen, was hard at work, leaned over into the left engine compartment. Junior Slava handed tools into hands that appeared. Obscenities emerged from the engine compartment and echoed off the trees, so things were apparently going well. Pyotr was most dangerous when he smiled and spoke politely.

Sergey waved to get Junior Slava's attention. "How soon?" he called softly.

Pyotr popped up and looked at him, trading Slava a towel for the wrench he held. "We could go now, Comrade Starshiy Lieutenant," he said quietly. "I would like to have a conversation with the *umnik* who designed some of these components, and perhaps punch him, several times, but *Valeriya* is sound. She will bear us home."

Sergey looked up at the sky again. "In the morning," he said, squinting through the snow. "You two get some sleep. Senior Slava and I will keep watch."

Several kilometers away, a blinding flash of light suddenly lit up the night, reflecting off the clouds bright enough that even Senior Slava emerged from his hatch to look. It only took a few seconds before it was gone, but Sergey felt a pain like a hot nail being driven between his eyes. He must have gasped and swayed, because Pyotr was suddenly there holding him upright. "Sergey?"

Sergey blinked rapidly to clear his eyes. The pain receded far enough to think. He took a breath and released it. Good enough. He was *Russian*. "Mount up," he called through gritted teeth, knuckles white on the hatch coaming. "We are going to investigate."

Senior Slava gave him a hunting smile. "Is that wise?"

Sergey smiled back. "No."

They laughed as the engines turned over.

Konradius checked his scanners again, cursing at whatever atmospheric and temporal conditions made the readings so confusing. Nothing in this century should be able to generate such static, unless the impending probability node was more complex than any of their theories had predicted.

Bad enough that the insertion bubble had been too small for anything larger than a man. He felt naked in only personal armor and mounted ordinance. Still, he only had to kill a single man, who would otherwise become the hero of the Battle of Berlin. With that single death Konradius could change the entire future into a place where his ancestors properly ruled. He would be a hero when he killed the great distant grandfather of *She* who had defeated them in the 24th Century *putsch*.

Konradius he smacked the scanner with one hand, hoping to knock free whatever gremlins had taken up residence in this time and place. He felt like a barbarian doing so. Aryan equipment was supposed to work in all conditions, even the distant past. Flight was out of the question too, if the scanners were balky. Snow would be a distraction if he got too high, and a fall would be potentially lethal if any of his other systems failed. He cursed harshly, found a rough bearing, and started to walk. It was just one man he needed to kill.

Konradius watched his scanner screen turn to the same static snow as the skies overhead. Overhead, the skies suddenly turned day-bright. A silent lightning bolt took shape on the slope, too bright for even his polarized lenses. He squinted until he had to close his eyes.

The daylight passed. And then a woman stood before him.

Of course. They wouldn't let the past go that easily.

Tatiyana took a deep breath and tried to lay still as she concentrated on the logogram. She felt it take hold, ink seeping into her bones and corners. Nobody had ever tried a leap this great before, but the apparent success of the death cultist's machine meant it was theoretically possible to go back into the deep past. Or their assassin had just leapt to his death between spaces and she was about to join him.

She considered what would happen if she failed her mission. All of this would be gone. Would never have been. Even if she succeeded, she would probably die there, trapped in the distant past, unable to power a leap home.

So this was death. The ending. Had her life been meaningful?

Tatiyana turned and looked at the face at her left shoulder. Her grown daughter, Katerina, smiled down at her, a single tear rolling down her face, but a smile of love and warmth echoing silently between them. A hand reached out and took hers, just for a moment.

Tatiyana felt that love engulf her as the others in the kin-group picked it up and reflected it. She drew the *breath of change* deeper into her soul. Around her, reality softened.

She watched as her kin-group focused their own psionic energies under her own as a stable platform from which she could launch. There were others here with more sensitivity, more range, more control, but none with more will.

In her mind, a tower as tall as the sky, with the logogram as the spear tip, dominating a perfectly flat, dusty white plain. She picked up that tower in her hands, herself suddenly as giant as the spire, turned it over, and plunged it into the ground. Reality opened beneath Tatiyana's feet and swallowed her whole.

Tatiyana fell three feet to the ground from the cold darkness between time. She landed like a gymnast, low and coiled. The air was ten degrees below freezing, so she automatically amplified her internal temperature to compensate. Her bodysuit could handle the rest, mottled gray and skin-tight over her spare frame.

Simultaneously, she pushed out her conscious mind to a range of over a kilometer, but it was not necessary. The assassin had apparently barely moved from where he had landed, so her leap was more accurate than the quickly-cobbled-together theory had anticipated.

Tatiyana regretted that she would never be able to tell her kin-group that they had succeeded, that she'd made it to the right place and time in the past.

Now she had to win, or they would simply fade out of existence.

Across the slope, the assassin raised a hand, holding a strange mechanical device. Always, the death cultist obsession with powers of the machine instead of affinities of the mind.

Her kin-group, *Zolnerovy*, Children of the Soldier, were much faster, much stronger, much tougher, a genetic inheritance they had shared widely across galactic humanity. The Death Cult believed in racial and genetic purity, and could only compete by using cybernetics and machines.

Tatiyana considered it a poor trade.

She considered the topography, the night, the weather, the trees, the century. Then, Tatiyana *moved*.

The death cultist, the time-assassin, was a mechanically-augmented human, and expected her to move like one as well. His first shot missed her by more than a body length, from a distance of only two hundred meters.

She smiled grimly. He would learn. He would compensate. He would get closer.

Tatiyana got closer as well.

# St. Georgi

Sergey's head finally cleared when they got to the place where the lightning bolt had struck. The fire had faded, but he kept his hands on the handles of the big *DShK* machine gun, just in case. Strange voices whispered in his head of dangerous intent and magnificent dreams as the tank rolled forward.

As a boy, Sergey had always felt a little strange around others. He had occasionally known vivid waking dreams, visions, that had always come true afterwards. As he grew older, he stopped telling people about them, and eventually they forgot the strange child, all but his *babushka*. She knew. She was a witch, a proper daughter of Baba Yaga. She told him so.

In war, those visions and voices had kept him alive. After three years together, Pyotr and the Slavas considered him lucky, and didn't ask or argue when he had leaps of consciousness or insight. Such kept them alive as well. Especially when their base had been attacked and overwhelmed by a surprise patrol of German tanks, three days ago. As far as he knew, they were the only survivors.

Sergey rotated in place, carefully checking every flank and the sky. Again, learned survival traits. They were alone.

Or rather, the Slavas and Pyotr were alone. Sergey had a new voice in his head.

She was not the girl in the park. This voice was deeper, older, than the petite blond Valeriya he had yet to meet in her park on a summer day in 1946. And this new voice called him *Dedushka*, grandfather, with an ironic laugh in her voice, as if she was much older than he.

She flashed an image into his mind. The death cultist, the future assassin with the strange pistol, firing at her. Sergey watched the treeline light up in rhythm with the vision.

She also warned him of the Nazis of this time, and their future plans for him. He watched an apartment building collapse under the impact of a shell fired by Senior Slava. He had never been there, had never even seen pictures of it, but he somehow knew the place. Berlin. A city dying in fire.

A chill reached his soul. Even the heat of both engines running could not warm him.

Sergey swung the big machine gun back and forth, checking that it traversed well. Hell was just over the rise.

Konradius cursed as he missed the girl again. He could not believe how fluidly she moved. It was almost like she was anticipating the shot. Could she? Was she reading his mind now? The mind-hider was supposed to protect his thoughts from the powers of the psionics. Had it failed?

He fired three shots in rapid succession, almost blindly. The first went well wide, the second hit in front of her. The third seemed to kiss her hip before she could evade.

A-ha! She was reading his thoughts. And now she was distracted.

Konradius triggered his power-vaults and leapt into the air at her. Hover-jets held him skyward as he closed the last fifty meters, savoring the agony on her face as she held the scorched flesh and tried to control the pain.

He laughed and tried to think conquering thoughts at her.

She looked up at him, eyes the size of saucers, like a meat animal meeting the butcher for the last time. Konradius smiled and centered his weapon on her face.

Tatiyana drew the *breath of pattern* into her charred flesh and concentrated on turning off the nerves in her hip. It was possible, but she had never been wounded so badly before. It would take time to heal. Time she did not have. The death cultist was closing. She looked up.

Too late. He was above her. Death was an instant away.

Time seemed to stop. Tatiyana watched the fingers begin to squeeze the trigger on his bizarre mechanical weapon. She reached out her powers and took hold of the trigger. A stray thought nearly made her giggle. A psi didn't need machines, could have killed her already.

She focused everything she had, pushed the *breath of still water* into his hand to prevent him from pulling the trigger. She heard his thoughts turn to rage. For good measure, while he was momentarily distracted, she caused the power-cell to fall out of the bottom of the weapon.

His rage caught fire. He dropped the weapon as Tatiyana clawed her way to her feet.

The pain from her hip was nearly blinding. It would have conquered any other of her kin-group.

Tatiyana would not be beaten. She envisioned the sky-tall spire again, grasped it in her mind, drew sustenance from it. Will. Defiance. Victory.

Across from her, the death cultist landed heavily, as if he could punish the very earth beneath his feet. With his left hand, the weak side, he drew a long knife, an alloy almost lavender, and advanced, howling curses in the old tongue. Why anybody but a death cultist would learn *Deutsche* was beyond her, but they all did. Perhaps it was part of an initiation?

Tatiyana was out of options. She could not run. His armor was too fast. She could fight him in close combat, but would lose to his augmented mechanical hardware in her current state.

On a normal day, she could augment herself as well. It was not an ordinary day. Her death was at hand. She had failed. The future would die with her.

But a voice in her mind *insisted. Demanded.* Will.

As she froze time to a crawl, Tatiyana reached out her senses, looking across space, time, probability. There. A good death. A relevant death. A memorable one. She skipped backwards two steps as the death cultist swung his blade horizontally at her. No. Not yet.

Sergey listened with senses other than his ears as they approached the crest of the hill. The voice was calm and implacable, like a Baltic tide on a summer day. He felt like the English king, Canute, on the seashore, facing that tide.

But these waters would not be satisfied with a demonstration of power. They wanted his soul.

Sergey drew a deep breath in, mastered it. He felt all of the weight of thirty-eight centuries take root on his broad shoulders, like the Greek Titan, Atlas.

His Russian soul laughed.

The vision in his mind was as sharp as a seascape by Aivazovsky. He looked down.

"Junior Slava," he yelled over the din, "load with armour-piercing, composite rigid." The loader actually stopped and blinked at him for a second, before turning to the rarely-used ammunitions. It felt good to surprise the man once in a while.

"Pyotr," he turned, "when we crest the rise, stop quickly and hold the brakes. Senior Slava, there will be a man in knight's armor and woman fighting. He is a fascist. She is a comrade. We must protect her."

Senior Slava's face grew even more confused and surprised than Junior Slava's. "With a tank gun?" he said, incredulous, "How is that even possible, Sergey? Use the machine gun."

Sergey felt a laugh bubble up and out of his mouth. The things he had seen today. "Slava, even the tank gun will not hurt the man. But it will be enough to distract him. I have seen it." They grew quiet. It was going to be that kind of battle. Good enough.

Senior Slava checked the round going into the breach. He looked at Sergey one last time. "We are going to protect a peasant woman by shooting at her enemy with the main gun?" he asked. "Sergey, you are insane."

Sergey smiled. "Perhaps," he said, "but *we* are not taking the shot, Senior Slava. You are." Sergey climbed back to his hatch to watch the future arrive.

Konradius swung at the woman again. She dodged, but slower than before. The wound in her side was enough. He could defeat her now. He smiled. Victory.

On a side screen in his helmet, the secondary scanner suddenly pierced the static. Apparently, defeating her would be enough to see the present and the future again. His shock nearly overwhelmed him as a new signal appeared, one large circle containing four smaller ones.

How was that possible? He only had to kill one man to change the past. How could all four of them be so closely bound up in each other's destiny?

Konradius ignored the wounded girl and turned to engage the new target. It was a primitive metal land vehicle, made primarily of steel and burning long-molecule hydrocarbons for power. He reached for his personal weapon and realized he had dropped it in the snow when the woman had disarmed it.

Very well, a monumental death. He reached for the plasma lance strapped to his back. There had always been the possibility that her kind, the *mind-rapers*, could push a fighting vehicle between spaces. He had come prepared. There was absolutely nothing in this century that could resist it.

Konradius brought the plasma lance to bear with his right hand and armed the weapon, awkward with the knife in his other. A sound caught his attention. The girl.

She was not as wounded as he thought, or perhaps was more desperate. She lunged at him as he pulled the trigger, knocking the beam weapon off center. It punched a hole through a nearby mountain range.

Konradius screamed pure rage, silent outside his armor but echoing in his ears. He dropped the lance and thrust the blade into her chest. Blood pulsed out around his fist and she collapsed at his feet. Dead, or very close.

Konradius looked up at a sudden flash of light.

Sergey watched the flash of the lightning-bolt weapon pass five meters to the left of *Valeriya*. The voice surged in his head, then begin to fade, like a migraine that had changed its mind at the last moment. Across the field, the fascist turned his knife on the girl and drove it into the hollow spot below her sternum. Sergey watched her falter. Felt her fall.

Below, a voice called out. Senior Slava, with an anger Sergey had never heard in three years of fighting. "Clear," he called. Junior Slava echoed a beat later. Sergey felt the future crystalize in his mind as Senior Slava pulled the trigger. *Valeriya* rocked back on her heels as she hammered her slug downrange, St. Georgi slaying the dragon.

Sergey would hold the image the rest of his days. Senior Slava's shot drilled the man in the heart. The armor held, but the round still had all the kinetic energy of a tank-killer. It picked him up like the kick of a Cossack horse and tumbled him several times through the snow.

"Sergey," Senior Slava called, "is he dead?"

"Maybe," he responded. "Reload anyway. That cannot have been pleasant." A chorus of rough laughs and rude jokes was his reply.

Sergey saw the girl move, badly wounded and bleeding to death. He grabbed the little medical kit they had cobbled together and leapt down from the hull to race to her. Behind, he could hear the whine of the turret as it inched around for a second shot.

Sergey felt her reach out and touch his mind as he closed, felt the voice fading. She tried to communicate something important, but could not. Instead, she crawled. Sergey raced closer, anything to save her life.

Thunder and lightning filled the night as *Valeriya* fired another round into the Nazi Templar, tumbling him several more meters but not breaking through the armored carapace. Sergey blinked to clear the spots in his eyes.

The girl stopped crawling and did something on the ground he could not decipher. And then she raised herself up on her elbows and pointed a thing that looked remarkably like a submachine gun at the fascist. A bright beam of coherent ruby light connected her to the Nazi for a split second, and then his armor finally failed. The fascist exploded, and then Sergey felt the shockwave reach him.

# Valeriya

Sergey rolled over, made it as far as his knees, and crawled to where the girl lay on her side, the strange knife still stuck in her chest. The blood around it appeared to be stopped, but there was too much of it, plus more coming out of her nose and mouth.

He knelt beside her and touched her throat to make sure. Beautiful blue eyes fluttered open and focused on him. He heard her voice, but her mouth never moved. It was in his head. She was the other voice.

*Dedushka*, she said. *It's really you.*

Sergey studied her closely. Dark hair cut short. A slender woman, long, nearly two meters tall, more than half a head above him standing. Muscled in a way that Russian women never were. She looked like one of Herakles's Amazons. Perhaps this was Hippolyta made flesh.

"Why do you call me that?" he asked. "Who are you? What are you?"

In his head, an insistent *push*. An image appeared. A family lineage tree, with an impossible number of generations. He saw his name at the top, shrouded in legend and fog. Another name, hers, far at the bottom. *Tatiyana*. A name charged with its own magical legends from other women in other centuries. Centuries? Really?

*Really*, she pulsed back at him. *I am your many-times-over grand-daughter.*

Sergey looked at the empty crater across the burned clearing. "And him?"

Another image. Two timelines, intertwined like the *Caduceus*, Mercury's staff. Others behind them, fading into infinity. *They believed that they could alter the future by changing the past. I was chosen to stop him.*

Sergey felt the voice fading as the girl, the woman more than two decades older than him who called him grandfather, continued to die in front of him.

*I only wish...* she trailed off.

"What?" he whispered softly.

*I would have liked to have met the first Valeriya, the Mother of our line. She was supposed to be here. This is where the legends begin.*

Sergey felt her reach into his memory and pull out the picture of the pretty blond girl seated on a Moscow park bench. *Valeriya.*

A sound made him look up. Pyotr rumbled the great steel beast closer and parked it. Junior Slava manned Sergey's machine gun as Senior Slava slowly spun the turret around, looking for an enemy to kill.

Sergey pulled off his glove and touched her cheek tenderly. Contact made her voice stronger in his head. *She is the second Valeriya,* he pulsed at her. *Let me introduce you to the first woman to bear that name.*

Sergey picked her up and stood, suddenly Atlas again, able to bear the weight of the heavens without flinching. Carefully, he held on to the spark he saw in his mind, her soul, and walked towards his friends.

Her spark was fading as he took her hand and placed it on the bow of the little British *Matilda* Infantry tank.

Her fingers traced the letters and he heard a voice in his mind whisper the name as she died, a happy, contented smile on her face.

*Валерия.*

# Tatiyana

The ground was too frozen to dig her a proper grave. It would not thaw until summer, at this elevation. Instead, Pyotr had proceeded to gather every stone he could locate in the area until he was satisfied. The Slava's continued to keep watch. Sergey held her slowly-cooling body close to his and wept frozen tears in the shelter of Valeriya's bow.

Sergey looked up as Pyotr finally approached. "Sergey," he said quietly, "it is time." Pyotr helped him to his feet and stepped back. They escorted him to the grave like an honor guard and watched solemnly as he laid her body on the ground and placed the first stone above her head.

"Her name was Tatiyana," Sergey said aloud, his voice harsh after so long silent inside his head. "She came here to protect us from evil. Let her be remembered as our guardian angel."

Sergey stepped back as Junior Slava approached and placed the strange weapon on her breast, as one would at a viking funeral. He added a second rock beside the first and stepped silently back.

Senior Slava stepped up, holding the strange purple knife as if it were a sword. Sergey had argued, very briefly, for putting the poniard in the grave with the other weapon, but his crew had mutinied and refused. Senior Slava placed it on her chest now as a viking would, and then lifted it and held it upright. He stepped back and took his place on Sergey's other side.

Pyotr stepped to the far side of the grave solemnly and picked up a large stone. He covered her face with the stone, stood, and stepped back, facing his comrades. "Tatiyana."

Senior Slava placed the blade in his hands with all the dignity of the King of England knighting him. "Tatiyana."

Junior Slava placed a hand on his shoulder to provide strength. "Tatiyana."

Sergey suddenly felt all of the weight of the heavens again. He would have fallen, but for the two Slavas holding him upright. "Tatiyana." Slowly, they guided him back to the other woman in his life and left him in her care while they helped Pyotr build a proper cairn, a decent burial.

Sergey carefully wrapped the strange poniard, insanely-sharp, in a spare shirt and placed it in a storage locker that had been welded to the outside of the turret, for safe keeping. After the war.

He put one hand on the cold steel of his mistress and let her strength flow into him.

Tatiyana had left some small portion of herself in him when she died. Even now, he could hear traces of her voice, and see flashes of a world far away across the chasms of probability. Her ghost might even haunt him for the rest of his life. But that simply made her another protector, to go with this one.

***Валерия***

*So, I accidentally committed literary science fiction. I even submitted this one someplace important, with the most wonderful rejection policy in literature. You send it in electronic. They promise to read it. If they don't contact you in 90 days, consider it rejected and move on. That you are reading this means that they passed. Shucks.*

*I want to thank Joel for considering the science and ethics of what I have proposed, and being a guest First Reader.*

*And now the weird part. The names have been changed to protect the guilty. And no restaurants (or zoanoids) were injured in the production, but the rest happened exactly like that.*

*It really was one of the weirdest Sunday mornings I've ever seen.*

# Myrmidons

Hive dreamed.

The world, the vision, was larger than simple dirt and grass. All tomorrow's roads stretched out before it, endless ribbons of bronze and chrome.

Some ended in fear. Others in winter. A few in the great sunlit distance of time itself.

Hive awoke troubled.

Before it, beyond the maze, an ending made of terrible, apparently-random chance, invisible to the workings of the simple creatures, had suddenly appeared. Hive could not deflect it, much, but perhaps enough.

The shadow was itself cast in shadow. But Hive saw the outlines in the middle distance. They were cast in concrete and steel, trench warfare and chemical munitions. What man/builder, the humans, mistook for *progress*. Hive had dreamed down that road and woke in tears, as only Hive could cry.

Hive composed itself before the tears could upset the harmonic of the Nest. Workers needed direction. Warriors needed purpose. Queens needed love. Thinkers needed dreams. Hive had dreamed.

Hive selected a Thinker, tasked her with *advocacy*. Hers to counter the case against future dreams. Hive selected a second Thinker, tasked her with *prosecution*. Hive put the case to both, went back to dreaming.

There was time before decisions needed to be cast into chemical communiqués for the Workers. It might be possible yet to deflect the river of time.

Hive returned from future dreams. Magnetic poles of opinion flowed back and forth between *advocacy* and *prosecution*, slow motion ripples of chemical tête-à-tête moving in semi-forgotten tides, responding to unseen celestial bodies.

Hive remembered the sea. Thinkers tasked with *memory* contained salinity, motion, destruction. Thinkers tasked with *observation* had mapped the celestial mechanics of the greater and lesser orbs. Hive had incorporated their theories of movement and ascended well above the Inner Sea that was not the barely-remembered Terrible Sea to escape the constant motion and occasional aquatic sublimation.

Hive was a grand-daughter of survivors.

Hive considered *advocacy* and *prosecution*. There were myriad long-term benefits to the dream. The pain, the sacrifice, would be exquisite. Hive would be without hands.

Short-term, stochastic probability could be trumped by black swans. Edge-probability dreams could be made manifest in windows too short to react meaningfully. Both *advocacy* and *progress* proposed contingencies and mitigations for the unthinkable as part of executing the greater dream.

Fulfillment of the modified dream required Hive to clone itself.

Hive considered the logic. It was unassailable. A war on two simultaneous fronts. Hive felt the tendrils of fear insert themselves into the dark corners of the Nest.

The risk of precognition was realized when time spent exploring long-term dreams left the Nest at risk of short-term annihilation. Hive had dreamt too long, seen too many futures, fallen into the trap of narcissism, of arrogance.

The present had intruded, in awkward, destructive advances, a hungry snake come hunting.

Hive polled the Thinkers.

The Nest was fat and happy with scholars. Large, urban predators and rose thorns kept the smaller ones at bay, protecting the Nest and allowing resources to be allocated into cognition and dreaming. Resources now at risk.

To clone or not to clone.

To suffer the beetles and spiders of unforeseen fortune, or take up arms against a dream of devastation, and by opposing defeat it.

To die. To sleep. Perchance to dream.

Or to awaken, having forgotten how to dream. To face the undiscovered country. That place beyond the dreams where the evening sky faded to dim distance.

Thus did precognition reveal the cowardice of dreaming, losing the name of action.

Hive considered the dream again, the risk, the reward, the *possibilities.*

Put forth explorers to live in the now, that Hive might, by chance, bear a daughter with the ability to dream. Visit the waters, salt and clean, at the bottom of both sides of the mountain. Find a way to communicate the dream.

Live.

It would clone itself.

Scout paused, tasted the plane of options in front of her. Soil had given way to rounded red stones, hot with summer sun and laden with man/machine flavors. The stones quaked with anticipation as man/machine approached, passed.

Scout dabbed her trail and moved forward, seeking soil beyond stone.

Worker considered duty. Such was paramount.

Her pathway was bright with footprints, limning direction, purpose, boundary. She followed her sisters forward, one half of one body length maintained, pace maintained, bearing maintained. Her sisters followed, half a length maintained.

She trod as a desert-bound camel, six legs dropping scent to reinforce the path, a chain of existence stretched out, fingers on a hand, thorn-canes brambled.

Duty.

Thinker touched another worker that passed the crest of the great mound and descended into the crevasse, turning her loose to seek food or useful resources. The path deltaed as search parameters activated in random patterns. Food-find.

Thinker had been selected for scholarly content that would guide the workers. There was no food here, as they would understand it. Without her, they would quickly traverse the available surfaces and return to the Nest, bearing little.

Thinker kept them scattered and working, a tremendous waste of energy dictated by greater needs. She contained the insight that she impersonated Loki as they explored the confines of Skrymir's glove on the way to Jotunheim. Thinker laughed at the esoteric subtleties.

Thinker had tasted both of the man/clothings when she set her scent trails. Two giant mounds of unknown material, tasting of cotton fiber, petroleum distillates, and Man-scent, awaiting her in the midst of a great space, a wooden plane dyed with seed extracts and sealed with other petroleum distillates.

Thinker had been assigned the task to keep the others localized and focused. A Scout would have quickly found the contained mountain of seed intended to venerate the avian species. Even a Worker could have wandered astray and begun to haul home the foodstuffs that later would have been available as spillage outside the great Temple.

Thinker was a herald. She touched another worker and activated her local-search behavior. Many strange things had been found, collected, and returned to the Nest, where they would be cataloged by future generations of Thinkers. It was good.

Scout tasted cotton. It was old and musty, dabbed occasionally with splotches of colored vegetable dyes in giant patterns invisible from so close. It tasted of man/clothing, underlain with food tastes. It was a favorable find.

Scout dove through gaps in the weave, seeking the dark, cool spaces underneath, prepared for ambush and death. The darkness might be home to beetles or spiders, possibly snakes. Scout proceeded with care.

The darkness was damp and solitary. Sterile.

Virgin.

Uncolonized.

Scout pivoted to retrace her steps, reinforcing the chemical road to guide more explorers. Hive must know of this place quickly. Perhaps Thinkers would come.

Scout quivered with excitement.

Hive considered the near-future.

Queens laid eggs at reckless pace, in anticipation of coming cataclysm. Thinkers transcribed chemical treatises on diverse topics for new Thinkers being born and initiated into the Mysteries. Workers scoured the great artifacts for food and resources, returning empty much less often than anticipated.

Hive considered the dream anew. The patterns remained barely-favorable. Perhaps the gods would find the sacrifice adequate and forestall the darkness. Hive could only hope.

Hive polled the Thinkers.

Aggregated Scout reports painted a landscape of other lands, already populated by natives of all sizes and postures. In any direction, expansion would come at the cost of warfare, a return to the primitive times before dreaming.

Man/machine scent lay heavy on the land as well, trench warfare and chemical munitions. Always in the shadows of the gods.

Thinkers rippled, calm waters subject to a fallen stone. Hive waited eagerly as the chemicals were digested to form a picture.

Man/cloth. Cotton burlap. Fresh soil churned with agriculture on the scale of the gods. Wooden fortress walls to keep ground species at bay. Unclaimed territory, as yet. A beachhead across the red stone plane. Hope.

Hive considered the two halves of future dreams. The *Sacrifice* to appease the gods. The *Colony*, that a daughter might thrive.

Hive polled the Thinkers.

Combined consensus counselled caution. But the Thinkers lacked dreaming.

The *Sacrifice* was necessary. The *Colony* was necessary.

Hive glanced once into oblivion, rolled the dice with destiny.

Hive issued the order to invade.

Thinker considered the impending quakes. It was not the lesser guardian. Her fear and disdain kept her clear of their caravans. No, this was one of the Giants, a titan of destruction, at hand. Perhaps even Skrymir himself, come for his brogans. Thinker considered her observations as Hive's plan advanced.

A shadow as grand as the sky cast a pall over the morning sun.

Earth quivered and groaned as the giant approached.

Worker-trail glossing the world as night-bound highways.

Thinker was tasked with *survival* and *observation*. A modern seer, she read the portents and warnings from the gods.

The message was clear. The time of sacrifice, of desolation, of loss. All was at hand.

Thinker abandoned her post atop the man/clothing, aware that the workers would not have enough time to escape. None of them would survive. Thus was it written, chemically inscribed on her soul. Thus was it dreamed.

The Titan approached. It was Skrymir. It was morning. It was time.

Thinker fled.

Every instinct, every road, every ley-line led back to the Nest, well-hidden outside the great fortress of the gods. Thinker fled away from the Nest, deeper within Jotunheim.

Thinker was tasked with *survival* and *observation*.

Man/giant/Skrymir lifted his brogans from the wooden floor to carry them to distant lands. Thinker leapt, fell several body lengths to safety. Thinker fled under a nearby wooden mountain and ceased all movement except respiration.

Man/giant/Skrymir was a visual hunter. Movement = death. Especially as angry as man/giant /Skrymir would become in mere moments.

Thinker was tasked with *survival* and *observation*.

Hive resisted the siren call of precognition. Too much risk rotated around the nexus of probabilities as they unfolded this morning. To dream of tomorrow would be to risk today.

Hive polled the Thinkers.

Hive had never encountered such behavior before. The Thinkers hummed with excitement and scientific squabbles. Whole bodies of knowledge were being ripped up and rethought, as workers brought back their artifacts.

Hive had never undertaken a systematic survey of man/cloth taste before, except to ascertain the tremendously low probability of foodstuff resources. With so little to find, workers had tasted everything, repeatedly.

Hive had actual man/cloth fibers with man/giant liquid essence contained therein. Thinkers consumed it, distilled it, fathomed it. Man/giant was much more complex than any had guessed. Far more so than the lesser and greater predators. Hive could spend years understanding the giants, their taste, their composition, their essence.

Hive dreamt of communication, rather than mere supplication.

It made survival, for herself, for her daughter, all the more necessary.

Hive tasked more warriors to the invasion, the colony. Knowledge must become immortal. Hive or her daughter must have time to understand. To dream.

Man staggered downstairs, not yet fully recovered from a hard work week, even with the benefit of eight hours of refreshing sleep.

The century-old hardwood floors creaked and groaned under his weight, a morning symphony as he approached the front door.

He must have been tired last night. His shoes were in the middle of the entryway instead of over in the corner with the rest. Man bent over with a groan and picked up his Merrills, looking for a chair where he could put them on.

Kittie sat on the back of the sofa and meowed once at the pigeons and squirrels under the bird-feeder out front, a queen atop her fluffy purple throne. She eyed Man with Cat-look, silently complaining that Man had not yet filled her food dishes.

Man blew her a kiss, the morning ritual underway.

Man sat in the dining room on the hard wooden chair, fresh socks on, and reached for his shoes. One foot went in, stomped down, settled. He stopped, unsure of the itchy-sensation. Man looked down.

Frantic Workers scurried in all directions from the surface of Man's shoe. Several attempted to climb man/giant in their frantic haste. He slaughtered those first.

Man removed his shoe, looked inside both.

Ants, everywhere. Tiny, black myrmidons on some unknown quest.

Man howled with rage, stomped off to his inner sanctum.

Man returned moments later, brushing stragglers from his limbs and crushing them.

He sought the entryway where the Merrills had spent the night, found the conga line. In through the hinge-side of the door, around the edge of the floor mat, pooled in a circle in the middle of the floor, a figure-eight of ant bodies frantically running for home.

Man brought devastation.

Mountain-bound Zeus raged. Lightning bolts of fury consumed whole companies of Workers at once. Liquid death from the skies, chemical rains that killed with a touch.

A lake of greenish death consumed the middle of the hardwood floor. Lightning bolts struck again and again.

Man opened the door, willing to invade the outdoors in stocking-clad feet in his pursuit of vengeance. The caravan-path followed the edge of the porch. Man smote them, again and again.

He cast his brogans into the middle of the porch, looked inside with horror, at the numberless invaders that had taken up residence. The voice of doom spoke, a monsoon of liquid vengeance pouring into every crack and crevasse, until there was no escape, no prayer.

Death.

Hive did not need the Thinkers to understand when the moment came. Hive had seen it, several times, in dreams.

The caravan-line of returning workers simply ended. The last worker returned, followed by nothingness.

It had begun. Now to hope that the gods would be satisfied with *Sacrifice*. Perhaps a third of the workers had been lost. Survival itself hinged on the vigilance of the warriors, and the luck of the scouts.

Would it be enough?

Man surveyed the battlefield, a dominant, victorious wargod.

At his feet, thousands of corpses, piled atop each other, twisted in death with silent screams of agony.

Victory.

Man eyed the strange pattern in the floor, an alien crop circle etched in drying poisons on the wood.

"Okay," he said, suddenly less than Ares, "that's odd."

Woman approached. "What is, honey?" she asked, Aphrodite in the morning sun.

Man circled the spot on the floor warily. "They ignored all the bird seed," he said, pointing to the bag just inside the door. "Left everything alone except to pile ten thousand of the little buggers in my shoes. Look at the floor."

Woman studied the patterns while Man went for water and paper towels and garbage bags in the kitchen.

Woman eyed him speculatively on his return. "That's the strangest thing I've ever seen," she said.

Man grunted in agreement as he knelt on the floor and began wiping up the charnel house of horror and devastation that covered the floor and front porch. It was something from the Vedas, writ modern.

Woman moved closer. "Need help?"

Man looked up, smiled. "No, I've got this," he said. "Why don't you go feed Kittie before she wastes away with hunger and turns feral?"

Woman departed.

Man cleaned up the battlefield, slowly, methodically, glancing frequently back at the spot in the middle of the floor, and the bag of birdseed.

Man looked up from his daydreams as Woman approached. "Ready to walk up and get breakfast?" she asked, surveying the now-cleared battlefield.

Man reflected on strange visions. "In a bit," he replied. "I want to take another shower and be clean before food. Kinda went overboard with the ant-spray."

Woman sniffed carefully. "I am so happy you got some with no scent this time," she said.

Man smiled and kissed her as he went upstairs to repeat the morning rituals.

Hive consented to dream.

A Thinker had returned. She had been tasked with *survival* and *observation*. She brought news. It fit within the parameters of the original dream.

So far, so good.

Man heard the phone ring as he dried from the shower. Murmurs followed.

Woman stood in the door to the bathroom. "It seems," she said, "that our *luck* is very good this morning. In spite of everything else."

Man looked at her, as confused as normal by all things Woman. "How's that?" he asked as he hung the towel on the bar and passed her with another kiss.

"That was Joann from the restaurant," she replied, face beginning to pale as shock and realization set in. "There was a terrible accident and they had to close."

Man stopped and looked at her, reading the signs and engulfing her in a hug. "What happened?"

Woman took a deep breath. "A car turned the corner too fast and plowed right through the front of the place." She stopped to breathe again. "Luckily, no one was hurt, because they always reserve that spot for us." Realization hit. "If we'd been there on time, we would have been sitting there. We could have been killed."

Man held her close, stalwart, resolute, loving, until the spasms passed. "My *fu* is good," he said simply, an old joke shared between them.

Hive polled the Thinkers.

The second phase of destiny had begun.

The beachhead that would become *Colony* was established, organized, defended. It was rich soil, freshly turned, laden with sympathetic nutrients. The daughter would be able to burrow deep, safe.

New Thinkers had been hatched and tasked with the *memory* and *understanding of planter boxes.* The daughter would be vulnerable for a time, then reliant, fractious, and finally independent. Warm communications would become formal, cold, ritual. Hive needed to catalog everything known about the land beyond the red stone plane before the daughter came into her place.

Several black swan moments had passed, as yet untrammeled. Hive began to hope.

Man looked up from his coffee. Woman had that look. He waited.

"I've been wondering," she said, aimlessly only if one was not paying attention. "What would the kids do with this house, if something had happened to us."

Man considered. Man danced right at the edge of understanding, unconsciously, before the thought fled before him.

"Probably," he said, "sell the place to developers. They'd knock the old joint down, level everything, and put in condos."

Woman scowled. "Over my dead body," she said.

Man shrugged. "Well, babe," he said, "that almost happened, except for the ants this morning."

Woman made a scared face. "I know."

Hive considered the day. Futures had been saved. Foreign lands colonized. Sacrifices made.

Scouts tasted new lands of man/machine. Workers labored. Warriors endured. Thinkers challenged scientific orthodoxy.

Quiet reigned.

Hive descended once more into the deep dream. Black swans could only be mitigated. Even now, new plans were being executed, contingencies crafted.

Hive wanted to touch that dim, distant land once more.

Man lay still, bathed in darkness.

Woman slept fitfully, eyes masked against brightness in the barely-fading evening heat.

Man recalled the feel of tiny hexapodal feet, feather-light, on his skin. He remembered a conga line of invaders, dead on the floor in that bizarre alien crop-circle. He considered that caravan, disappearing under the front bushes, an entire house untouched, cat food, bird food, people food. Only his shoes. His shoes.

Man eased from bed silently, lest Woman wake. Kittie eyed him sleepily, as always.

He carefully trod the old steps down, close in to the side where the boards didn't squeak. Out the front window, he considered the rose bushes.

Time passed.

Man retired to the kitchen, looked around. He grabbed an apple and a knife, reduced spherical geometry to trapezoidal symmetry.

Man considered.

The front door was silent as he opened it. He walked, a night ghost. The night air was cooler here, down among the green.

Man traced the caravan trail in his mind, stopping in front of the semi-feral rose bush that kept the cats and squirrels at bay. Carefully, he parted leaves and branches with his free hand, placed the apple slices on the dirt in his own alien crop circle, eating the last slice lest he mar the accidental *fung shui* achieved along the way.

Man straightened up, reflected. He shook his head at his superstitious silliness, retired, hopefully unseen, into the darkness.

Upstairs, silent dreams of lazy summer afternoons overtook him.

Hive awoke from her dream. Smiled.

That distant afternoon sun was filled with many daughters, reaching from water to water in both directions, myrmidons marching into the sunset.

Scout transcended the *Colony*, crossed man/stone/concrete and found a line of death/demarcation protecting other giants.

Worker carried her load on strong feet, a taste of strange berry from a distant land to feed a queen.

Warrior stood fast.

Thinkers argued on the nature of apples.

*Dieselpunk. That wonderful era of pulp science fiction from the 30's and 40's. A time of technological wonders playing out on the radio: airships, bullet trains, mad scientists, lantern-jawed heroes, and damsels in distress. This story was inspired by those old radio operas, but updated with some more exotic possibilities, because, really, what's the fun of doing this if I have to stay within all the old conventions instead of telling it more like it probably would have been.*

*I'm already planning what happens in Sarajevo. Hopefully, Volume 4 will contain more of Tor and Dead-eye's adventures in saving the world. If not, perhaps there is a novel in their future.*

# Moscow Gold
## Chapter 1

Dedirick entered the bar with a quick moue of distaste. His dapper tweeds were ever at odds with the sorts of ruffians that populated these seedy, dock-side establishments. Still, he was driven by purpose. Needs must, and all that folderol. Dedirick sighed internally and strode forward.

He considered the dive, one of his favorite haunts on the waterfront. A vast expanse of mirror on the bar back with many decorations: a faded, three-years-out-of-date 1935 Normal Rockwell calendar next to a Boston Braves pennant. Picture of a British Line-of-Battle-Airship flying low over Boston Harbor on a cloudy day. Possibly the *Swiftsure* but hard to tell from here. A poster from President Smith's 1932 re-election campaign, next to one from President Roosevelt in '36.

Wood floor and copper-topped bar scarred by generations of workers. Bottles in every shape and flavor of alcohol. People in every shape and flavor of Irishman.

Dedirick eyed the crowd carefully, professionally, but without lingering anywhere where unwanted attention might instigate hostile reciprocity. At thirty-eight, he was really too old to keep getting into so many bar fights. Honestly.

Dedirick waded carefully through the mob, eyes on the prize. The locals were a rough lot, but polite. He wasn't exactly an outsider here, just not an Irishman.

There. At the back of the bar, where it tucked in for a short lateral, just enough for two seats. And the seat beside her was currently unoccupied.

Like so many girls of her generation, her mother had named her Victoria, for all the obvious reasons. But that was before the Great War, and the world had been a more innocent place then. However, she was never a *Vicky* as a child. Too rambunctious and energetic, forever skipping and running and asking. Her father had taken to calling her *Torie* instead. Much more fittingly appropriate for such a girl, and a wonderful play on his own Liberal politics. The man still had a wicked sense of humor.

Grown to womanhood, she remained *Torie* to her close friends, but was also a force of nature, a grand opera without all the girlie weeping bits. An adventuress. Now she introduced herself to people simply as *Tor*. He approved. It suited her.

Tonight, Tor sat at the bar, resplendent in a white Brooks Brothers shirt under her battered brown leather jacket. Porcelain skin. Carefully red nails. Long, thick hair that hinted at dark chocolate, pulled back and braided to stay out of her way. Ever practical while still remaining a woman of beauty and substance. He smiled, just because.

She arched a perfect eyebrow at him in greeting as she drank from something caramel dark in a highball glass on the rocks.

Dedirick planted himself in front of her and managed a good harrumph. "I do wish, my dear," he said, very nearly drowned by the noise, "that you would get out of the habit of having cryptic telegrams delivered to my office. You are beginning to make the Managing Editor nervous."

She eyed him over her glass, took another sip of her whiskey. "Dedirick Carlyle. Finally. Hello, Teddy. I wouldn't need to do that, Dead-eye," she said caustically, "if you were ever in that office." Her accent was purest London smooth, as were her manners. "Would you like a drink?"

Dedirick felt his moue return. "Tor, darling, I am a reporter," he said plainly. "It is my job to be out and about. I find out whatever needs knowing by being on the street listening and asking. And would you please stop calling me that?"

Her smile in response started tart and warmed slowly, like the iced whiskey she drank. "I will point out, again, Dedirick, that that is how you spell it. Dee-Eee-Dee-Eye-Rick. And it is appropriate."

He scowled. Not too heavily. She did have a point, after all. "And I will remind you, again," he began, "that I only had to shoot Lady Fausta because she was about to throw you off Observation Deck of the Empire State Building. Had you listened to me in the first place, we would have never gotten into such a crisis."

Her shrug was more eloquent than most people could have achieved with a paragraph and a brace of speech-writers. It was an old discussion. He watched her take another sip.

"So, my dear," Dedirick said, "what adventurous need draws me down to dock-side on this blustery evening?"

Dedirick waited patiently as she took a long drink and gathered her thoughts. Or stretched out the moment to make him squirm. He was never sure with Tor. No one was ever sure with Tor. She preferred it that way.

She finally turned her upper body to face him squarely. It brought her entire presence to bear. The impact was magnetic, almost physical. Her voice was so low as to be almost a dream. "The freighter 'Carrion Crow' entered the harbor this morning. The airship, *Sharkoliya*, hasn't been seen, yet." She did not smile.

Dedirick felt the blood drain from his face. "Velitchkov."

She nodded and took another sip of her whiskey. "Precisely. I need you to find out why."

He staggered to the empty stool and signaled the bartender. "I believe," he husked, "I will have that drink, after all." *What devilment were they up to?*

Tor pulled a pack of French cigarettes from her jacket pocket for a couple of quick taps on the bar. She put the first cigarette in her mouth, flipped open her maroon Zippo lighter, and leaned into the flame.

Valdís snapped the lid of her chrome Zippo lighter closed as the tobacco caught flame. It had been a long day, just getting this far. There was still the night ahead of her. She drew a lungful of the harsh smoke and felt it energize her as she gave her blond bob a flip to get it out of her face. Her current eyepatch was a rose worked into the leather and dyed blue. A gift from an admirer.

The red glow of the cigarette reflected in the glass of the bridge window as she looked out over the deck and checked the night watch below. The *Carillon De Cannes* was mostly dark at this hour, with just a few bridge lights around her and deck lights below. A silent, iron beast at rest.

Outwardly, she was just another battered cargo ship, no different than many others in Boston's Inner Harbor. The few, weak, lights on her deck showed occasional movement as she rode at anchor, awaiting a wharf opening so she could dock and disgorge her cargo. Perhaps tomorrow, perhaps in a few days. A few people came and went on the deck, intent on some task.

Up close, the deck had a rough, unpolished look. Welded repairs showed rust instead of fresh paint. Oil and grease had dripped from the deck cranes, leaving slick spots that never seemed to disappear.

The ship itself gave the impression of *seedy*, in a way that objects never seemed to manage, at least, not like neighborhoods could. Perhaps it was a neighborhood, a place, a thing. The *Carillon* made the whole harbor seedier just by being there. Valdís had known enough seedy neighborhoods to be sure. She smiled at the thought.

For a moment, Valdís watched the lights of East Boston flicker off the bow. She could see the point on the horizon where the Sumner Tunnel emerged, hauling people to Jeffery Field. Somewhere beneath her, she knew, a giant mechanical mole was slowly tunneling, burrowing a new bullet-train tunnel under Boston Harbor that would connect the Boston-Montreal corridor with another one to Halifax. Eventually, it might render transports like the *Carillon* extinct, but the world was always going to need smugglers. Far easier to do that hiding in a big cargo ship, than on a train.

Valdís checked the night once more as her cigarette burned down. A sailor stood watch on the bow beneath her, bundled against the stiff harbor wind. She knew his nose had been broken at least once, leaving a perpetual scowl as he watched for movement. She approved. A British machine pistol was slung from a shoulder strap, somewhat hidden behind his back from the casual watcher, but immediately at hand if needed. She had seen him use it before. The ship would be secure. She nodded to herself.

Valdís opened a side hatch from the bridge to the walkway outside, spilling light onto the deck. The man on watch glanced up, nodded to her. Valdís nodded back and flipped the last remains of her fag overboard before she stepped back onto the bridge.

She checked to make sure the hatch was sealed tight before she crossed to the rear of the cabin and descended the stairs. The eyepatch on her left side always made the stairs a little tricky if she actually paid attention, so she kept her good eye on the corridor at the bottom of the stairwell as she moved, playing out the movements in her mind if a gunman were to suddenly appear from a hallway below.

She reached a hand down and touched the wooden handle of her Mauser pistol, more for luck than expectation. She traced the cord hooking the butt of the pistol to her belt. The weapon was slung low on her thigh in a special holster that showed off the rose design carved into the sides of the magazine well and inlayed with mother-of-pearl.

The movement and touch brought a small smile to her face. It never hurt to be prepared to deal death at a moment's notice. Such planning had kept her alive this long. Others had not planned so well.

At the bottom of the stairs, she traversed to another hatch and entered the wardroom. She scowled professionally at the assembled crew before she spoke. The boat lived and worked in English, but that was a second language to most of the crew, so the babel of accents sounded jarring, especially her own. Nobody else spoke Icelandic, however, so her innermost thoughts remained her own, even when she forgot herself and muttered aloud.

She looked around disdainfully as the hum of voices quickly died down. "We are secure," she said, barely above a whisper. Forcing them to listen to her reinforced her place as Velitchkov's second-in-command.

Valdís took her seat next to the Captain and studied the men around her. It had been almost two years since she had had to shoot any crew members to make a point. It did not appear that an object lesson was necessary. At least, not tonight. Tomorrow would take care of itself.

She watched Captain Velitchkov take a sip of black coffee from an ancient tin mug as he waited. The man had a cruel face, thin and sardonic with a bushy, black mustache jutting out from under a previously-broken nose and crow's feet etched indelibly into the corners of his eyes. On his head, the classic captain's peaked cap with the Skull and Crossbones logo worked in gold. On one ear, a big gold hoop earring. Truly, he looked the part of a Hollywood-cast pirate. She approved.

Valdís watched him smile cruelly at the crew as the silence stretched. Finally, he set the coffee mug down and looked out over the assembled mob of killers and cutthroats. "Very well," he said, his harsh Bulgarian accent echoing strangely from the metal walls. "Here is the plan."

It was another seedy dive. Dedirick suspected he was going to get his fill of them before this adventure was out. At least this one was known for the quality of the breakfast they served. All the fishing captains started their mornings here, hours before sunrise, right out the back door and down the long wooden dock.

Dedirick located his prey at the bar, dabbling at a plate of bacon and eggs and the morning edition of *The Grand Banks Express*. The older man looked up as he approached.

"Good morning, Allan," he said affably. "How's retirement treating you?" Dedirick slid onto the stool next to the weathered captain.

Allan settled his paper and took a bite of bacon, eyeing the newcomer sidelong. He sighed. "I find boredom to be the great foe, Teddy." A sip of coffee followed the bacon.

Dedirick nodded. "Regret selling the *Lady Ellen*?"

Allan smiled wryly. "Right up to the moment," he grinned and tapped the paper, "when I read the weather forecast this morning. Nasty squalls down from Canadian Maritimes. What brings you out this early, Teddy? Or up this late?"

Dedirick signaled the waitress for a mug of coffee. He waited until she departed. "I have heard a rumor that the *Carillon De Cannes* was in town." He took a sip of the black java and waited.

Allan stirred finally. "Nobody has seen the airship *Sharkoliya* in nearly a year. Perhaps Velitchkov was killed?"

Dedirick shook his head slightly. "Doubtful. Tor's rifle wasn't big enough to penetrate her belly armor over Togo." He thought back for a moment, "And the storm that came up, combined with the smoke generators, probably let him get away safely. All we did was rescue the hostages."

Allan let the moment hang. "Always a win. Have you talked to our *friends* downtown, yet?" He looked down into his mug of coffee.

Dedirick studied his own coffee as well, as if the answers were there in the grounds, like they might be in the tea leaves. "Not yet," he replied. "Their first words will be to activate the old network." He sighed. "I decided to start the task early."

Allan laughed quietly. "Time," he said with a gruff smile, "to get all the old warhorses back into harness? Aren't we getting a little long in the tooth for this sort of thing, Teddy?"

"We beat the Whites back and saved the Revolution, Allan," Dedirick smiled back quietly. "Now we have people like Tor to carry the banner forward. We just have to help her beat the fascists."

Allan raised his coffee mug like a wine glass and a toast. "Careful, Dead-eye," he grinned evilly. "You may rouse me to song if you keep this up."

Dedirick rolled his eyes. "Just as well I'm leaving, you old fart." He rose, slid a quarter onto the counter. "You couldn't carry a tune in a fish bucket."

Allan's basso laugh followed him to the door.

Valdís glanced back as she heard the butler's footsteps approach the great mahogany door. The broken-nosed crewman, Orne, sat in the front seat of the rented car, polite and seemingly-diffident. But she knew he had one hand on the machine pistol, hidden under a newspaper. She smiled enigmatically to herself as the locks surrendered noisily. Roses on either side of the mansion's porch filled the air with a sweet taste of home.

The door opened slowly to a tall, burly man with an English face in a dark suit and an accent from the Eastern Midlands. "May I help you, madam?" The tone stopped just short of condescension in that particular way that only the English had ever mastered.

Valdís considered her own attire and decided that perhaps she rated *madam* after all. Long legs encased in dark nylon tights and black leather pumps. A speckled gray knee-length skirt with a matching fitted jacket, buttoned to the neck. Black leather gloves. She had even taken the time to add makeup this morning and her most decorative eyepatch, the one with the rose emblem worked into the leather in bronze. Truly, a cunning disguise.

She pulled a business card from the outside jacket pocket that was too small for a gun and handed it to the man. "Valdís Eydísdóttir," she said, quiet, eloquent, sharp. "Here to see the Vizconde."

She watched the man inspect the calling card briefly and then inspect her, first professionally and then as a man, in two separate sweeps. She considered turning so he could inspect her bottom as well. It was enough to distract many stupid men. She refrained.

He glared silently at her for a moment longer, as though he could read her thoughts. "Yes," he drawled slowly. "The Princess of Death. You are expected." He stepped back and gestured her in. "Please relax in the salon and I will notify his eminence that his guest has arrived."

The man led her to a small but very elegant sitting room, comfortable for two, cozy for four. She listened to his hard heels recede on the marble floors and inspected the room for clues about the man she was meeting.

The bar was fully stocked, with over fifty bottles in various states of dismemberment. Two comfortable leather chairs that looked well-used and well-kept. A leather sofa under the east-facing window. Three bookcases filled with leather-bound volumes on a random collection of topics. There was not a fleck of dust on any of them, and not a single spine showed where one had ever been opened.

Valdís nodded to herself. A typical Spanish nobleman, wealthy and well-bred, and probably only barely literate. A man of passions and excitement rather than intellect. In short, a fool.

She glanced at the walls to see if there were any pictures of him in a matador's costume from his younger days. Yes, there. Not bad looking, either, forty years ago. Perhaps he might have a son who was accidentally born with his father's looks and his mother's brains? Or a daughter. She smirked at the thought.

Footsteps echoed down the grand staircase. Two pair. The heavy clomp of the butler, and a lighter stride in his wake. She moved to stand behind the lesser leather chair with one hand on the back, figuring to use her femininity as a weapon. She missed her Mauser.

The butler shadowed the doorway briefly to confirm her presence. "Madam," he rumbled quietly, "El Vizconde." And then he stepped back and disappeared. She listened closely, but the man made no sound whatsoever, so either he was exceptionally skilled or lurked just outside the door. She shrugged in her mind and turned to the man standing in the doorway.

The grandee was very much a bantam peacock. Her heels gave her an two extra inches of height over him, beyond the three she would have had barefoot. He was dressed in a red and gold silk affair that lingered in that vague no-man's-land between the matador costume from the pictures and a lady's pajamas. El Vizconde's leonine halo of hair had gone mostly white, and his nose showed the strain of decades of dissolute living.

But the eyes were sharp. Valdís saw layers of cunning in them as the Vizconde took her measure at the same time. He had the hints of cruel smile as he approached her.

"Maravilloso," he whispered as he approached. "You honor me to have such a stunningly-beautiful woman in my salon."

Valdís waited patiently as he took her hand, bowed over it, and kissed it lightly. She supposed she might have taken the gloves off before he arrived. Or not. She was here on business, not seduction, regardless of what this dandy thought. But she was also here to charm him, so she allowed him to hand her into the lesser chair, and accepted a glass of red wine, while she waited for his patter to bleed out like a shot pig.

"So," he finally came to the point. Valdís tuned back in to what he was saying, confident she hadn't missed anything beyond vague bluster and subtle innuendo. "Velitchkov will be ready to transport my cargo on Tuesday?" His eyes had turned card-sharp.

"Indeed, Vizconde," she said as she set the barely-touched glass of wine down. "The freighter *Carillon De Cannes* is anchored in the Inner Harbor now, while we finalize details."

He leaned forward, suddenly attentive. "Not the airship? Would it not be faster?"

She settled back in her chair and crossed her legs demurely. His eyes drifted south as she spoke. "The *Sharkoliya* would be much faster, yes, but when you are smuggling several tons of gold bars into Germany, it is far better to maintain a very low profile." She breathed once to draw his eyes slightly higher. "The gold will make it to Hamburg in good time. It will quickly turn into tanks and aircraft to support Franco." Truly, the man was a badly aged violin she had no intention of tuning.

Valdís watched him take another deep drink of his wine. From the breath wafting over her, it wasn't even his second glass this morning. She held her breath as best she could.

"That is good, Senorita," he mumbled. "The Communists must be stopped. The world is discovering that Democracy is a failed experiment. The Socialist revolutions must be thwarted at every turn. Fascism is the wave of the future. It is the natural order of things."

Valdís smiled politely as this *creature* patted her hand and ranted. It paid the bills. And provided her people to kill regularly, although she understood now why Velitchkov had insisted that she dress up for this little charade. Yes, an attractive woman for the old fool, but she also had had to leave her Mauser in the car, when she would have been tempted to shoot the man on general principle.

When he stopped to draw in a fresh breath for a new tirade, she leaned forward suddenly. "And when will the shipment be ready for us to pick up, Vizconde? There is much planning to do to get ready."

The man blinked, apparently unaccustomed to female conversation more complicated than pillow talk. "Uhm, Tuesday. I believe I said Tuesday." He paused, marshalling his thoughts sluggishly. "Perhaps Monday, although some of the others are still wavering in their commitment. Their names will be remembered, when the revolution comes."

She nodded respectfully. It seemed a useful placeholder. Valdís rose to her feet in a sudden surge that caught the old man off guard. "You have been most helpful, Vizconde. Until Tuesday."

She held out her hand to be kissed again as the man stumbled to his feet. "Must you depart so soon, my dear?" he asked in a rather plaintive voice. "Will you not join me for brunch on the terrace?"

"Alas," she smile hollowly, "my duties prevent it." And you can have your fourth glass of wine this morning alone, old man, and leave the intrigue to professionals.

Valdís stepped to the door and found the English Butler patiently waiting out of sight. She nodded to the man and followed him to the front door in unbroken silence, resisting the urge to wring her hands. She needed a shower.

# Chapter 2

Dedirick paid off the cabbie and listened as the taxi sped away. A few buildings and a simple sign indicated the Gould Farm Airport. He pulled the latest of Tor's enigmatic telegrams from his pocket and read it again. *Framingham?* Yes, this was the place. Wherever the hell this was.

He shrugged and started towards the large hangar. The zenith sun just barely warmed the early March day. He suspected rain.

The transition from sun to gloom blinded him as he stepped into the great bay door of the hangar. Dedirick paused for a moment as his eyes adjusted.

*"Bonne journée, mon ami,"* a warm alto voice trilled at him from the shadows.

Dedirick blinked several times and squinted. He could barely make out a figure hunched over a table, working with jeweler's lenses and a file to shape a piece of metal. She had flipped the lenses up on her forehead as she smiled at him.

"Abena-Marie," he smiled as he took a long stride towards her. "What are you doing here, so far inland? I was expecting you to be on the water. Tor told me she had finally found a replacement for *The Swan.*"

He embraced her as she rose, kissing her on both cheeks to say hello, and on the lips because she was a beautiful woman who would allow it. She allowed it. And assisted for a moment before she stepped back.

"Oui," she said, her soft French accent contrasting so nicely with her milk-chocolate skin. "Mademoiselle considered ze new Sikorsky, ze S-43, to replace the lost 38, but in the end, Douglas made her a very good deal on one of their DC-3's. After that, I haff made some interesting modifications for her to make it a much more useful aircraft."

Dedirick started to say something, but became aware of a dull roaring sound in the distance. He turned. "What the devil is that?"

Abena-Marie stepped up beside him and put her arm around his waist to turn him. They looked out over the open landing field. "That, monsieur, is Mademoiselle Torie, returning from a quick test flight to seat in some new engine parts."

"But what is that sound?" Dedirick looked skyward futilely.

"Ah," she said with a warming smile. "English-style jet turbines. I have improved the basic design some for a better fuel burn rate. *Hank* is on her downwind."

Dedirick finally spotted the aircraft as it suddenly exploded into view on his left. He was familiar with the basic DST and the DC-3 models, even painted Italian racing red, *rosso corsa*. Someone, he suspected Abena-Marie herself instead of a machine shop, had removed the powerful radial-piston engines, and the propellers, and replaced them with what he could only describe as Buck Rogers rocket engines slung under the wings. The sound was an overwhelming leonine roar as the aircraft banked tightly, low to the ground on base and final approach, and then flattened out and swooped in to land from the far end of the grass field, as graceful as a duck settling to water.

Dedirick started to take a step forward to meet the airplane, just Abena-Marie grabbed his arm and held him back. She tried to say something, but it was lost in the noise. Finally, the sleek Italian race car swung in sideways and the roar cut to a high-pitched machine whine before finally dying to silence. Dedirick thought his ears might have popped, as well.

"Now, Monsieur Dedirick," Abena-Marie leaned close to whisper in his ear, "it is safe."

He followed her out. As they approached, Tor leaned out the window and waved, shutting down the great aircraft methodically before getting out of her seat.

On the nose of the airplane was a portrait of a beautiful woman with similar eyes and hair to Tor. Her given name was elegantly scribed across the bottom, but nobody ever called Tor's grandmother Henrietta. To Dedirick, and everyone else, she had always been *Hank*. It fit her far better. It fit the plane as well.

He walked slowly to the rear of the craft, examining changes to the DC-3 he knew. Finally, he reached the rear and waited on the right-hand side for the hatch in back to open. Behind him, Abena-Marie carefully popped open a panel on the low-slung pod beneath the wing, the *English-style jet turbines* that made so much noise, and tinkered.

Up close, he realized that the landing strut in back was longer than others in this class, raising the tail higher than normal while resting. After a few minutes, just as he was beginning to grow restless, Dedirick heard a metallic ping and watched a ramp wind down on hydraulics at the rear of the craft. Tor appeared, backing a machine slowly down the ramp as he sprang around to assist her.

It would have been charitable to call it a motorcycle. It looked nothing like the old Henderson he had once owned, nor the Indian he still rode occasionally. For one, it was far too long, with a wheelbase nearly three feet longer than his Indian, a result of a long set of front forks that ran out at an acute angle and flat, curved handlebars.

The rear wheel was all wrong as well, being nearly treadless and almost flat, with a rounded edge. On his Indian, the rear wheel was a hemisphere perhaps six inches across. This was nearly a foot wide.

And the engine was strange. It was not the v-shape that many modern motorcycles had adopted, nor the horizontal powerplant from his old Henderson. Up close, it resembled nothing so much as the seven-cylinder radial engine he had once seen on a biplane outside of Marrakesh. If it was, the machine would be capable of an utterly asinine top speed.

He supposed that the longer front forks made sense from that standpoint, as it would keep the center of gravity extremely low. The machine would not be particularly maneuverable at speed, but nothing would keep up with it on a flat straight-away, except the aircraft it had arrived upon.

Dedirick looked up from the machine to see Tor studying him with almost the same intensity. "What have you found, Dead-eye?" Her voice purred, but there was still an edge of wild energy and danger underneath it. He paused for a moment to compose his thoughts.

"Given," he began, "the amount of noise and rumor generated in this town just by the asking, I have learned a great many things from a great many people. And you should make sure to avoid the Verdun Dinner Club tomorrow evening." He moved along as Tor pushed the machine towards the great hangar behind him.

"Why is that?" she asked quietly. "Trouble?"

Dedirick shrugged. "A once-promising political career will be destroyed by a sex scandal tomorrow night. Some people will want to be seen being seen. Not people you would benefit from, either way."

She shrugged in turn. "Darby would prefer it that way, as well."

Dedirick approached the question carefully, obliquely. "And how is your husband? And his father, the Baron?" One never knew, even if there was never a hint of scandal.

"Both are well," she said, nonchalantly with a warm smile. "I was home in time for Saint Steven's Day and stayed three weeks. Darby is busy with Parliament, as always. The Baron and Baroness may outlive us all."

Dedirick filed that tidbit away with a smile and a nod. "The other news seems to agree on a meeting between Velitchkov's assassin and a certain ex-patriot Spanish Viscount."

Tor made a moue of distaste. "Valdís. Again."

"Indeed," Dedirick replied. "The Spaniard appears to be fronting for a cabal of wealthy American businessmen with fascist tendencies. There is a rumor of gold being smuggled, possibly to Hamburg, possibly to Cadiz, to support the Nationalists. They have had extensive contacts with many of Hitler's people, so we are unsure as of yet." He enjoyed watching the way her head snapped up at that last morsel.

"Have you," she drawled slowly, but with immense intensity for such quiet words, "talked to our friends downtown?" The words hung in the air like the scent of lavender for a few moments.

Dedirick felt, rather than heard when Abena-Marie stepped up close beside him. She wore a subtle, flowery scent, one that promised tropical sun and rolling beaches for a lucky few. Tor only dressed up when required by societal pressures.

He smiled back at the chocolate beauty beside him, her face tense, and threw in a wink. He still owed her some level of teasing from the last time, when she had spent an evening pretending to be his well-born French wife. He turned back in time to catch Tor's roll of the eyes.

"I have," he said simply. "They would like a meeting. I have an address and a time, this evening."

Tor's face was unreadable. "Well," she replied. "Let's not keep them waiting."

Something about the blue Mallory sedan coming around the corner caught her eye. Valdís lived on her instincts, and her left hand was inside her pea coat, wrapped around the butt of her Mauser, in a heartbeat. The car trolled slowly down the street, as if the driver was looking for a parking space, but she wasn't fooled.

Movement in the passenger seat caught her eye. The man in the dark fedora lifted a machine gun with a drum magazine into view and tracked her as she took two quick steps and turned sideways behind a majestic elm tree.

There was a roar that sounded like a demonic typewriter. Valdís could feel the bullets impacting the other side of the tree. A stray round shattered a plate glass window storefront behind her. A woman began to scream.

Valdís drew the Mauser from under her arm and dragged the hammer back with her long thumb. A quick peek around the tree drew more attention from the homicidal woodpecker in the sedan. She ducked back, drew a breath, and kneeled.

She had counted the driver, the gunner, and a third person in the back seat. Valdís leaned out again and fired once. Wood exploded above her as an incoming shot creased the edge of the tree. Downrange, the passenger bucked as if on a wild horse and put three shots into the street before his dead fingers released the trigger.

In response, the sedan suddenly accelerated. Valdís put her second shot through the back-seat window and watched the rider in back slump over.

She rose and waited, holding a breath close. At the end of the block, the sedan turned left. She smiled and raised her right hand, connecting a line between her eye, the gun-sight, and a point on the horizon. She breathed out and snapped the trigger three times in rapid succession. A hole appeared in the driver's door. The driver's window shattered. The driver slumped out of sight.

She lowered the pistol and held it close to her hip as she listened. Around her, people were just now beginning to react and make noise. From around the corner, she heard the crunch of steel as the Mallory drifted into parked cars like a derelict barge. A car horn began to sound, as if a dead man had fallen his entire weight against it.

She smiled, dropped the safety block, and lowered the hammer on her Mauser. She tucked it carefully back into her shoulder holster and slipped around a nearby corner at a brisk walk. A knit cap, pea coat, and eye patch would make her too recognizable in a few moments.

She crossed the next street and ducked into an alley, emerged three blocks away, and flitted into an apothecary. Out the back door, she stepped up to a gray coupe, popped open the door, and slid into the seat with a tart, "Drive."

Orne turned the engine over before he glanced her way, and didn't rumble a question at her until the car had eased away from the curb. She pulled the knit cap from her head, letting her blond hair catch the light, and traded her eyepatch for a pair of darkened lenses.

"The Italians," she replied to his rumble, "are still a touch put out about Portsmouth, it would appear." They shared a harsh laugh.

Tor kept her attention focused on the howling machine-beast between her legs as she barreled down the road. The bike was very smooth, but very loud, which was just as well, as Teddy was being very deliverate about keeping his weight centered on the seat behind her.

She grinned as she felt his hands, wrapped very carefully around her waist and clenched tight atop her navel, oh-so-careful not to wander. Her grin expanded to a smile. He wasn't half bad looking either, if she had liked boys. Not that she would tell him that. Tor opened the throttle and listened to the radial engine scream as she laughed out loud.

Behind her, Teddy leaned forward to yell in her ear over the din.

"Two streets up," Dedirick shouted in her ear to be heard, "and then turn right and go about a half mile."

Tor nodded and slalomed around a slow farm truck like a California Chaparral Cock. She decided to be nice and slowed down to a marginally-safe speed as she took the corner, rather than laying the bike into a low skid and making Teddy panic. He would have never complained, but she was feeling good. She downshifted for power as she straightened the black beast out and roared down a barely-paved country round originally cut by cattle. Danger and wind filled her.

Three blocks out, she cut the engine and let the sound fade. They coasted in silently towards the farmhouse. The big machine was remarkably smooth and stable this way, something Abena-Marie had tweaked with the rear suspension was working out. Perhaps they should patent it and make a fortune. Another fortune.

Tor smiled at the thought. Abena-Marie's father was a Rothschild and she had inherited more family money than even Tor had, from either the Lemieuxs, or the Beauforts she had married into. Still, money was possibility. Maybe she should buy a big ocean-going freighter and turn it into a mobile base, like Velitchkov had done. It had promise. And style. She could use a personal aircraft carrier at times.

The house was quiet. There was an old flatbed truck on the side and a newer four-door sedan parked in front. Darkness was fast approaching, and light spilled from behind closed drapes in the front room.

Tor braked the beast and flipped down the kickstand. Behind her, Teddy dismounted and straightened his suit while she removed her riding helmet and goggles and hung them from the handlebars. She started to take a step, but Teddy held her back.

"A moment, my dear," he said, drawing his old semi-automatic pistol from inside his jacket The gun was already loaded, cocked, and held safe with a simple flip switch, a trick he had apparently picked up during one of the wars he had done.

"Are we expecting trouble?" she asked tartly.

He smiled at her, broader but no taller, and generally far less physically imposing unless he decided to turn it on. "We are never expecting trouble, Tor," he replied, "but Velitchkov is involved, so that means that Valdís might be about."

She teased him with a grin. "You could have shot her, you know. I've seen you shoot women before."

Tor watched as Teddy straightened himself to his full height, towering perhaps half an inch over her in mock outrage. "I don't shoot people in the back. You know that."

She stepped to one side and gestured Teddy to precede her. "Monsieur." The grin was irrepressible.

She unzipped her leather jacket as she followed him to the stairs. The sedan was a non-descript navy blue that left no clues as to its origin. The truck would mean even less. These people were experienced professionals.

The building itself was an old farmhouse that had been absorbed by the village around it. It was a square box with a porch that wrapped around to the right, an unlit second story, and dormers looking out from an attic.

Teddy mounted the stairs silently in front of her, so she did the same. She caught him by a sleeve and leaned close to whisper, "Maybe next time you should try kissing her instead."

He glowered sourly at her for a moment and leaned close. "Or you could," he whispered back with a tease.

It got quiet. Even the crickets subsided. In the ominous silence, she heard Teddy flip the safety off as she moved to one side. He reached out and knocked on the door, three short, sharp raps. A pause. Two more.

From inside, she heard chains and bolts recede. The door opened with a rough, "Quickly," whispered harshly.

Teddy stepped through the tiny gap. She followed. The door closed firmly behind her.

Dedirick sized up the group in the crowded front room. Polzin, he knew. Nikon Evgenyovich had been his contact for years with the Reds. The other man seated on the couch was a surprise. Dedirick knew him by face, but had never spoken with him. The man was a spy. The other three were obviously muscle.

Dedirick nodded to the gentlemen seated and stepped to one side as he holstered his pistol. "*Tovarichi*, Mrs. Victoria Lemieux-Beaufort," he said with a wave. "Tor, Soviet Consul Kaminski and his assistant."

The two men rose. Kaminski kissed her hand English-style, while Polzin shook it firmly in the American manner. They returned to the couch as Dedirick and Tor seated themselves in overstuffed chairs. The goons kept a close armed watch on the doors and windows. Dedirick approved.

The silence hung. Dedirick leaned forward and put his hands on his knees. "Just," he asked, "how much gold is involved, that the embassy would take notice?"

Polzin and Kaminski exchanged a glance. Polzin shrugged eloquently with a tiny smile.

The Consul cleared his throat. "We believe," he began, with the faintest hint of an accent, "that the fascists have accumulated enough bar stock to fill a large truck. Approximately one and a half tons of metal."

Dedirick whistled. "Not nearly enough to offset the original Moscow Gold the Republicans transferred in '36."

"*Nyet*," Kaminski shrugged, "but enough to buy many tanks and aircraft and potentially alter the balance of the War for Spain's Soul."

Tor was leaned back, draped across her chair in what appeared to be a calculatedly- unperturbed pose. "And they are going to have Velitchkov smuggle it to Spain for the Nationalists?" Only her eyes betrayed any interest. They twinkled.

Polzin smiled like a cat. "If it was legal," he said, "they could have hired anyone to do the job. Your interest in the Bulgarian is well known. As is your history."

She smiled back. "And the limits of your assistance?"

Teddy watched Kaminski tent his fingers like a college professor contemplating a very-bright student. "The current Administration," he said, "is generally friendly, but there are many counter-revolutionary elements and tendencies at work. There have been talks of coups and armed insurrection to overthrow the progressives."

Dedirick leaned forward with a serious mien. "The economy is too good for revolution to succeed. People have grown fat and rich."

"Only because the progressive elements of the left are currently ascendant," Kaminski nodded at them. "Consider what might have happened after your so-called *Black Friday* in this country if the reactionary forces had prevailed instead of Keynes."

"They probably would have driven the economy into the ground," Dedirick shuddered, "and taken the rest of the world with it."

Again, Kaminski smiled. "Yes," he said simply. "A great and terrible depression. And they would have put the October Revolution at terrible risk. Scared and hungry people are more than willing to support dictators against the march of history." He turned back to Tor. "But we were talking about supporting your endeavor with the Bulgarian."

Tor leaned forward, eyes sparkling. "Where is the gold now?"

The two Soviets shrugged. "We do not know."

Dedirick cleared his throat. "I have it on good authority," he began quietly, "that the shipment is being assembled on the Viscount's estate." He smiled innocently at the sudden, shocked looks. "Friend of a friend, you know."

Dedirick watched Tor suck in a quiet breath, saw the wheels begin to turn in her mind. "How long," she said, "until they are ready for Velitchkov?"

Dedirick shrugged in turn. "Three, perhaps four days."

He watched her turn on the charm. It was like watching the sun come up. She speared each of them with a look. "Here's what I will need, gentlemen..."

Velitchkov eyed the estate disdainfully as the rented sedan circled the big cinder drive. Spanish nobleman with a fetish for rococo architecture and an overabundance of money had yielded a rambling orange mess that reminded him of a cake that had partially collapsed. The inhabitants were equally impressive, from his memory of previous trips. He sneered at the suit he was wearing as well. It made him look like a fop, or worse, a diplomat. And who threw a cocktail party on a Monday?

The car rumbled slowly up to the front door and ground to a halt. A goon dressed like a trained monkey hopped up to meet the car, and opened the door with a hard look inside. Velitchkov could see the bulge of a pistol inside his buttoned up jacket, right where he could never get it out in an emergency. Amateurs. Velitchkov stepped up out of the vehicle and pulled his suit straight.

Another goon pretended to protect the front door, standing to one side with a clipboard. Velitchkov stepped up and eyed the man for a right cross. He needed a drink soon, before he lost his temper at this silly charade.

The man looked up helpfully, as if he had at least half a brain. "Yes, sir?"

Perhaps a few body blows after the punch distracted the man. "Velitchkov," he said.

The man looked down his list, checked names, and nodded. "Ah," he smiled politely. "Welcome, Captain Velitchkov. El Vizconde is inside. About half the guests have arrived and are having drinks on the back patio. Will you need a guide?

Velitchkov gave the man a sour look. "I know the way," he said as he stepped around and entered the failed cake experiment.

Inside, the same polished marble tiles and medieval armor suits in the grand foyer. A carpeted staircase rotated to the right and lifted up to a mezzanine overlooking the grand space. Giant portraits of Spanish dandies shared space with the armors. The English Butler met him a few steps into the hall with a highball glass of whiskey.

"Captain Velitchkov," he said quietly, "the Viscount would appreciate a few minutes of your time in the library if that would be acceptable."

Velitchkov took a good drink of the whiskey and let out a slow breath. Finally, someone who had an understanding of how things were done. He nodded gratefully and followed the silent giant through a door under the staircase.

The library was obviously someplace El Vizconde rarely visited. It was too clean and subtle for the man. Built-in shelves of books were filled with leather-bound editions and well-selected bric-a-brac. Velitchkov would have bet that Spaniard had inherited the room and left it completely alone, save for the enormous portrait of himself as a young bull-fighter, back when Spain still had an empire.

A warm fire lit the room. Velitchkov watched the Spaniard rise up out of chair with a pineapple-sized snifter of brandy in one hand and reel a step towards him. The words came out in enough of a slur that this was not the first bottle opened today.

"Captain Boyko Velitchkov," he said happily, "it is good to see you again."

Velitchkov nodded politely at the Spaniard as he approached. For all his foppishness, the man represented a great deal of authority with the sorts of people who hired him to perform easily-deniable tasks. Alienating him would mean going back to smuggling opium in the Orient. "Vizconde."

The Spaniard walked very close and put his free hand on Velitchkov's elbow and clinked glasses with him awkwardly. "The last of the gold will arrive with the guests tonight and be packed up for you and your homicidal sidekick to carry onward to Germany. Quite a clever trick, no? Having a party as an excuse to bring all the principles with all their gold together. We will drive the communists into the sea. When will you be ready to travel?"

Velitchkov nodded sagely. "The rest of my crew will arrive after dinner," he replied, "so the guests will not be alarmed. Will it be safe?"

The Spaniard smiled up at him. "Of course," he giggled as he took a deep drink. "The General's people have sent over a number of guards to protect us."

"Yes," he said, "I have seen your guards, Vizconde. But I will feel better when the gold has arrived on my ship and been safely stored."

Another deep drink. Velitchkov was amazed at how much liquor he had seen the man consume at a single dinner and remain functional. Tonight would be another. "All will be well, Captain. You will see. Now, we must join my other guests."

On the back patio, Velitchkov found himself almost completely underdressed. But that was normal. He refused to even own a tuxedo. Too much risk of turning into these people. Still, he allowed the Vizconde to lead him out into the sea of people, like a Christian on his way to meet the lions.

Valdís smiled from the passenger seat of the baby blue sedan she had made Orne steal for her. She glanced over at the big blond gunman man with broken nose, but he was focused on the winding roadway. And rarely verbal at the best of times.

It was one of the reasons she usually chose him to drive her. Juan-Marco had never learned to actually shut his mouth for longer than five minutes. Lars was only interested in talking Swedish politics. Orne was quiet until he needed to let his Bren do the talking.

She glanced at the truck following them closely. It was too dark to see anything but headlights, but the dozen men in the cab and bed would be enough to take care of the shipment and see it safely to the port. And if more Italians showed up to argue, all the better.

The sound of Orne down-shifting brought Valdís out of her murderous daydreams. They had circled the Vizconde's estate to the dark side on the back of the hill and were approaching a shadowed break in the tall brick wall they had been paralleling.

Valdís reached into her pea coat and drew out the Mauser as the sedan turned into a small driveway and stopped next to a guard shack. She held it low at her side, next to the passenger door, as Orne rolled his window down. She glanced to her right to make sure nobody was trying to sneak up on that side before looking at the guard emerging from the dark doorway.

The man carried a long-barreled .38 loosely in one hand, but carefully did not point it at the car. She would probably have shot him if he had.

This would be when she would spring the ambush if she was in charge. But she was also far more dangerous than these *children* ever considered being, for all their bluster. She thumbed the safety off, anyway, just in case.

Valdís ducked down enough to make eye contact with the man. "The password is *toreador*," she said, keyed up.

Outside, the guard nodded and stepped back. He walked to the wrought-iron fence and wrenched the rusty iron handle open with a loud squeal. Valdís winced as she watched him stuff his pistol into a jacket pocket. Where did they find these people? She knew schoolgirls with better tactical acumen. Granted, she had taught them, but still, there was principle involved.

She thumbed the Mauser's safety back on and prepared to slide the pistol back into her shoulder holster when something caught her attention. Instinct held her poised. She heard death whisper.

At the gate, the guard had frozen, looking into the estate with slack-jawed disbelief. Oncoming headlights limned him like a halo. A roar of engine filled the sudden silence.

From inside the fence, a big flatbed truck appeared. It had the appearance of an army vehicle, with blackout headlights and a dark canvas cover over the bed. It accelerated forward down the slight incline, engine howling.

At the last moment, the guard dove back into his little shack. The truck slammed into the half-open gate and sprang both wings ajar like Moses. Orne stalled the sedan. Valdís considered her options, grabbed Orne, and pulled him down below the steering wheel, even as she threw herself headlong into the footwell on the passenger side.

And then the big vehicle hammered the sedan like an avalanche of anvils, sideswiped it hard aside like a linebacker, and was past.

Valdís cursed. Dead-eye had been driving the flatbed as it went by.

# Chapter 3

Dedirick used his best put-upon sigh, not that it would gain him even a carat of sympathy from Tor, once she had her mind made up. What else was new?

"Why," he said again, "can't you take Abena-Marie along on your little adventure?" He continued to put on the navy blue jacket she had handed him, and the silly little knit stocking cap that went with it.

Tor smiled at him tightly. "Because, Dead-eye," she retorted, "you're a much better shot."

He eyed her speculatively. "She's a better driver," he said, suddenly deeply suspicious.

"Indeed," she said. "But I need her testing out the new crash harness she has devised for me tonight. If it works, we'll sell it to various air corps as a new safety feature for pilots and make another fortune."

Dedirick turned his head far enough to look at her sidelong. "You already have several fortunes, Tor. What's the story?"

She grinned innocently at him. "Why, Teddy?" She batted her eyelashes at him innocently. "Whatever do you mean? That's God's honest truth."

He managed a good harrumph in her direction. "One of these days, young lady," he said evenly, "you will play it too close to the chest one time too many."

She gave him a serious look, finally. "Dead-eye," she said calmly, "these people are experts at the ancient Oriental game of *Go*. It is a game of space and planning." She zipped up her chocolate-colored leather jacket and headed toward the door, stopping to grab an oversized cloth satchel. "I'm playing stud poker. It's a game of people."

He pulled the hat down on his head and followed her out. At least he had taught her how to play poker well.

Outside, they found a taxi waiting. She smiled at him as she climbed into the back seat. "I had considered," she said as she slid across the bench, "getting an invitation to the Viscount's party and having you escort me."

"Wouldn't that represent a small problem, if you were there to steal all his gold?" Not that he hadn't considered doing the same. There were always ways.

"It would," she agreed. "That's why we are breaking in instead." He watched her pull out a small wallet and pass the driver a $100 bill. "Good evening, Manny. You have the address?"

The cabbie tipped his hat with a smile. "Yes, Tor."

She leaned back. "Good. Make sure you buy Shirley something nice with that."

Manny laughed as he slipped the idling car into gear and eased away from the curb. "Will do, ma'am."

Tor eased the door of the cab open silently and stepped out, staring at the brick wall of the estate. She slung her gear bag and fished from it a small black automatic pistol that she slid into a pocket and a set of lockpicks. It felt good to be here tonight, taking the battle directly to the bad guys instead of waiting for them.

She turned to Teddy. "Ready for trouble?"

He opened his jacket to show her the butt of the old Government Issue. "Planning a wild shootout?"

"The Viscount's staff," she smiled at him, "as you have pointed out, are much more for show than security. Considering the kinds of people the man has invited to this soiree, I expect most of them will be up at the house, keeping expensive things from wandering off."

As the taxi rolled quietly away, Tor led Teddy a hundred yards the other way, following a stout brick wall overgrown with ivy. It was less impressive now, poised on the verge of spring. There was almost no smell beyond the basic hint of decay from a long winter. It reminded her of Glasgow.

A dragon's mouth gaped out of the greenery, a pitch-black pit waiting to devour her. Tor peeked in and then stepped into the alcove. She kneeled and inspected the heavy wooden door. The keyhole was an even darker inkwell in the shadows. She went to work with the picks.

The space was in almost total darkness, but key, she knew, to picking a lock like this was touch, so light was unnecessary. She had learned this trick from one of Teddy's friends at a poker game. Hold the pick just so. Press the pins up and hold them out of line. Listen. Touch. Move to the next one. So easy.

So not happening.

"Crap," she whispered, apparently not quiet enough.

"Problems, beautiful?" She smelled Teddy's aftershave as he leaned closed.

"Frozen stiff from the winter," she replied, "maybe rusted." She pushed harder at a pin that refused to budge.

"So," Teddy whispered, "what's on the other side of this door?"

Tor thought about it for a second. "I think," she said, "a gardening shed and an abandoned greenhouse."

She felt his hand on her shoulder, pulling her back slightly from the door. The picks came away with her. "Perhaps," he said, "I have a solution." He smiled down at her.

Tor rose to her feet silently and gracefully. She held out the picks, but he shook his head and drew the automatic from his shoulder holster.

"You're not, I pray," she murmured, "going to shoot the lock, are you?"

He grinned at her. "Not at all, Tor. Not at all."

She stepped out of the way. "All yours, then, Dead-eye."

She watched him take a half-step back and brace himself. He stepped forward and kicked the lock with his bootheel. The frame shattered around the lock, spewing wood fragments as the door slid in perhaps a foot before stopping hard.

Dead-eye stepped back and waved her forward. "Madam," he grinned, Cheshire.

"And just where," she inquired, mock-serious, "did a respectable reporter learn that trick?" She stepped into the opening to glance around the door. From the pile of mulch wedged against the back of the door, it was obvious that it had not been opened in years. Teddy's voice floated up over her shoulder.

"Robbing banks," he replied smugly. "Especially in Petrograd and the western Caucasus."

She arched an eyebrow at him. "I know of a bank robber originally from the Caucasus. A Georgian fellow named Yusuf."

She heard Dead-eye flip the pistol's safety off as she slipped around the door into the darkness beyond. "Yes," he turned serious. "Him."

Inside the estate, Tor found herself in an abandoned quad bounded by a storage shed, a dead greenhouse, and a small cabin where a groundskeeper probably lived, when a previous owner had cared about such things. Now, the cabin was padlocked shut, the shed's door was half ajar, and glass panes in the greenhouse had fallen askew. Tor found herself standing on half a foot of accumulated muck and grass. She was momentarily offended, but then remembered who and what she was dealing with.

Apparently, this was the forgotten corner of the Spaniard's estate. Across the darkness, several hundred yards away beyond a formal garden gone to semi-seed, she could see a well-lit and well-kept patio and yard. Snippets of music from a string quartet wafted down the hill, along with the dull roar of crowd noise from the Viscount's garden party.

Tor slid the lockpicks back into her satchel and looked around for the carriage house. Teddy ghosted up beside her with less noise than a church mouse, a sudden wall of muscles and solidity by her left elbow.

His face had transformed. Gone was the reporter's open sociality and smile. In its place was a harder profile, etched like granite and weathered. He held the pistol low against his thigh with easy care, weight rolled forward onto his toes. She smiled to herself, and, when he glanced over, expanded it to him. Abena-Marie was a genius with engineering and technology, but the young Franco-Fanti woman was a mechanic.

Dead-eye, for all his protestations to the contrary, was a killer when he needed to be. He might need to be, tonight. His scowl softened. He nodded at her. A force of darkness and violence, carefully harnessed. Her smile turned radiant and then she smothered it into seriousness.

Time to annoy the fascists.

Tor headed to her left, down a walkway that time had not erased. Trees and deeper darkness marked the carriage house, carefully kept dark tonight so as to not disturb the Viscount's guests. She imagined that the rear of the estate, with rows of trees and no light, would look like the sea on such a moonless night.

She had to glance back occasionally to be sure Dead-eye was still behind her. The man made absolutely no sound, even in heavy, steel-toed boots walking on cinders and gravel. She was quiet as she moved. He was silence itself. The darkness swallowed them as they moved downhill and across the estate.

The carriage house slowly detached itself from the greater darkness, a great lumbering hulk of red bricks, surrounded by a circular driveway, and the several layers of hedges, all designed to obscure it from the greathouse above. It was quiet as she approached, Teddy her shadow. Several windows had been painted over, leaving only a lonely bulb over a side door to cast a pool of light.

She stopped at the rear corner of the building, a long blank wall. She considered the lockpicks in her satchel, then realized that the door probably wasn't locked. Why would guards need to protect themselves? She smiled and slipped around the corner.

The door was original to when the carriage house had been constructed originally, fifty or more years ago, and had contained carriages instead of automobiles. It hung loosely on its hinges, and even spilled a little light at the top of the sill from where the building had settled over time. The lock was even worse, a simple round hole for a brass key with oversized pins. The Viscount really believed in his invincibility, apparently.

Tor considered the door and pulled on fine leather gloves. No reason to leave any evidence. She already had alibis arranged, just in case. And what fool would complain to the police that someone had stolen gold it was illegal for him to possess in the first place? She considered petard hoists and had a silent laugh.

She glanced over as Dead-eye moved up beside her. She held up a finger to forestall another kick and closed her hand on the brass knob. It turned with oily smoothness and opened on silent hinges. A slice of light spilled out for a moment as she slipped in. She felt Teddy's heat right behind her, but he made no sound.

Tor stepped forward and closed the door as soundlessly as possible behind them. The great barn was utterly silent. She turned and watched Dead-eye move deeper into the building. It was like watching a shadow detach itself from her feet and drift off like fog. She followed in his wake.

Pride of place in the garage went to an immaculate phaeton limousine. It was a land-whale in chrome and black, sleek and refined. The flatbed military-style truck parked next to it looked dowdy and vaguely seedy by comparison, gray, with a shipping company logo on the door. A thuggish bodyguard, if you will.

Tor committed the name and logo to memory. Either Velitchkov had new friends in town or had started another company as a fence. Perhaps a visit to their office was in order. Or an anonymous tip to some of his competitors. She smiled an evil smile.

Dead-eye had moved to just outside the half-open door to an office. She watched him kneel down low and peek around the frame almost at the ground as she closed the gap. He remained frozen for several seconds before standing suddenly and stepping into the doorway, a low rumbling laugh emerging from his chest. Tor followed in surprise.

In the office, the chauffer was hunched over a table with his head down and tremendous snores echoing off the walls. A mostly-empty bottle of cheap gin lay on its side on the table near his head. Two more dead soldiers rested on the floor nearby. The smell was nearly solid. Tor was glad she hadn't eaten before leaving tonight. The stench was almost overpowering.

Dead-eye stepped close and poked the man with his empty hand. He looked up at her with a disgusted face. "Leave him like this?"

She wrinkled her nose and considered her options. "You know," she began, "if we tie him up and hide the bottles, they might not find him until morning. Keeping him from getting fired might mean he's around if we need to do this again sometime."

Teddy smiled at her and grabbed a spool of wire from a nearby shelf. "As you command, mistress." He safed the pistol and slid it into his holster as he went to work.

She rolled her eyes at him, turned, and walked back to the garage. It would be criminal to damage the phaeton, but she didn't want to leave them a vehicle for pursuit. She settled for popping open the hood and stealing the distributor cap.

She looked up as Dead-eye emerged. "He might be able to gnaw his way out before the apocalypse. Perhaps. We may need to send them a message to untie him in a day or two if they haven't found him by then."

Tor closed the hood of the phaeton carefully and gestured over her shoulder. "You have more experience with trucks like this. I'd like you to drive."

Teddy nodded, still in his serious place, and moved to the back of the vehicle. She watched him climb up and disappear under the canvas cover as she moved to the garage door. At least this had been modernized, with a large garage door in the middle that had taken the place of the two middle bays and part of the wall above them, with only the original outer doors, both barely wide enough for the phaeton, remaining.

Tor checked the chain and pulled the pin that held the door down. Behind her, the big diesel engine rumbled to life as Teddy kicked the starter pedal. He flipped on the running lights and leaned out the window to give her thumbs-up. She leapt up, grabbed the chain as high as she could, and let her weight start the spool to roll it up.

Behind her, the truck inched forward as he dropped it into gear, a greyhound quivering at the starting gate. She cycled the door as fast as the mechanism would allow and watched the truck roar past as soon as it had clearance.

Tor followed it out and sprinted to the passenger door as Teddy turned to his right and aimed it down the driveway. She climbed up on the running board, popped the door open, and climbed in. This model had an automatic transmission, so Teddy was concentrated on the road instead of his gears.

"Well, nuts," he said suddenly.

"What is it?" she said as she pulled the door closed.

"We've got company," he replied simply, eyes locked on the gate rearing up before them.

Tor could see the gate half open, with another guard standing in the middle of the driveway, staring at them, a deer in the headlights.

Beyond the man, a dark sedan and a truck smaller than theirs were taking up most of the driveway.

"What do you think?" she heard him yell over the roar as he mashed the accelerator to the floor. The big diesel jumped forward with a sound like a dive bomber.

She considered the two vehicles. "Velitchkov," she yelled back. "No time for subtle."

He turned to smile at her. "My thoughts exactly, beautiful. Hold on."

Tor braced her feet on the dash to absorb the impact.

The guard dove out of sight, just short of being run over.

The big diesel hammered into the gate, springing it wide open with a crash.

Dead-eye threaded the needle with the metal beast, shattering the passenger mirror on the building as they went past, and politely side-swiping the sedan, bouncing the lighter vehicle carefully out of his path.

The other truck was smaller, more of an oversized pickup than a two-and-a-half-ton military flatbed. Tor braced her hands on the roof of the cab as she felt Teddy swerve slightly to his right, away from the second truck, before turning the wheel hard over and striking his smaller prey just behind the driver's door.

Mass mattered.

Metal shredded, all of it off the lesser vehicle as it encountered the modified I-beam that comprised the big truck's front bumper.

Tor watched the smaller vehicle capsize like a yacht in a bad squall. The noise was almost painful.

And then they were past. The big diesel bounced a few times, rocked a little, and then sat right back down. Teddy cranked the wheel over and sped up the street. The sudden drop in noise was almost silent by comparison.

Tor relaxed her death-grip on the cab. "Let me guess, more bank robberies?"

He grinned at her, frog-faced. "Not at all, madam," he yelled over the engine noise. "Running rum in Maine. A very precise job."

She nodded. There were still holes in Dead-eye's past she hadn't filled in.

Velitchkov's nerves were already stretched thin from an hour of small talk with diplomats, financiers, and the kinds of parasites that attached themselves to that level of money and power. Disdainfully-intellectual men and the sorts of wives they accumulated, either connected blue-bloods or vacuous bimbos. Occasionally, both.

He slipped away from the current conversation on the relative value of the French system for administering colonial possessions versus the English method and grabbed a glass of something, anything, from the tray of a passing waiter. He made a good dent in it and contemplated making a run for the hors d'oeuvres table in the corner.

Dinner wouldn't be for another hour, at the very least, and you could float a destroyer in the amount of alcohol that would be consumed by this group in that period. He had already made enough connections for illicit goods and services to keep his team occupied for at least another year. He needed a break. Punching someone sounded far too good at this moment.

Velitchkov made his way through the big French doors and out onto the patio. The group here was quieter, or perhaps more spread out, and represented the lesser players: lawyers, doctors, politicians. A string quarter was ignored in a corner. A famous writer held court on his latest novel in another corner. Velitchkov made his way the other direction.

He needed some solitude before braving the mess that would be an alcohol-lubricated dinner with these people. Valdís would have been more interesting to send in his place, while he waited at the wharf with the ship, but she probably would have murdered one or more of the fools inside by now, for an ill-considered comment or wrongly-placed hand.

The thought of her in that group, a shark swimming with cod, brought a smile to his face. Perhaps he should bring her next time, dolled up in to her most elegant, made up and saloned by professionals, towering on heels, poured into a skin-tight top, gown sliced to the thigh, with her favorite knife concealed in her garter belt. Oh yes, someone would end up embarrassingly dead. And they might stop treating him like the hired help responsible for taking out the trash.

Tonight, it was bad enough he seriously considered going straight. The money would be much worse, but he wouldn't have to deal with this particular crew of fools and buffoons. It had its appeal.

A voice behind him heralded more pain. "Ah, my dear Captain," El Vizconde boomed out. "There you are."

Velitchkov was amazed that the Spaniard was still functional. He himself would be in an coma after that much alcohol. He might not have had that much to drink this year. Still, it was money. Velitchkov pasted a neutral smile on his face and turned. For good measure, he clicked his heels together and nodded formally. Little things went a long ways with this man.

"Vizconte," he said. Quiet, polite, subservient without being servile. Not that the man would remember, but others with his ear would.

"Are you," the Spaniard began, paused to hiccup once, and then forged ahead, "are you enjoying our little repast, tonight?"

"Very much so, *Senior*," Velitchkov replied. "Everything is excellent this evening, thank you, again for having me."

The Spaniard moved close and took a friendly hold of his elbow. "And how soon will your lovely assistant arrive to take charge of the shipment? Will she be joining us?"

Velitchkov smiled to himself while maintaining a neutral face. "Unfortunately, no," he said. "Because of the seriousness of this mission, one of us was needed down below to supervise things. Perhaps next time she can join your party and I will organize the men."

He started to say something else when a sound interrupted him. He turned and stared into the darkness below. It sounded like someone had dropped a metal shop off a cliff.

Beside him, the Spaniard's face took on muddled confusion. "What in heavens was that?"

A second sound filled the night, an explosion of iron, like metallic titans warring. Boyko considered he options. "I believe, Vizconde," Velitchkov said, "that I will be unable to execute your contract for transport after all."

The Spaniard rounded on him fiercely. "What are you talking about? You can't back out now!" His voice had risen to almost a scream.

And awkward lull settled over the conversation on the patio. Heads turned their direction.

"It appears, *Senior*," Velitchkov's voice dropped to almost a murmur, "that someone has stolen your gold."

Dedirick felt like the big deuce-and-a-half, the gray military truck, was an extension of his being, the way of a well-trained horse. It had been years since he had pushed a vehicle this big to the very edge of turnover and failure. He felt more alive than he had since Budapest.

He turned off the dark street below the estate onto the wider avenue where the hack had dropped them earlier. The truck labored up the incline. The engine was willing, but there were two boxes the size of coffins in the bed, filled with large gold bricks, and that much weight made it a chore.

The look on the nobleman's face would be priceless when he heard. Perhaps it would be appropriate to investigate an anonymous tip in the morning, just to rub salt in the wound. Certainly amusing. How would they explain the loss of that much gold, after the mere possession was made illegal in '33? Dedirick smiled serenely.

It didn't last long. In the surviving side mirror, he saw a vehicle barrel around a corner behind him in a noisy skid. It looked like a strange walleye, with one headlight true and the driver's side light cocked at a bizarre angle. He must have made them very angry.

"Tor," he yelled over the noise, "we might have trouble."

She looked over at him with concern. "What is it?"

"That," he pointed a thumb backwards, "is probably Valdís."

Valdís rode out the earthquake as the sedan bucked and bounced.

A moment later, the world seemed to end in a tremendous steel symphony, counterpointed with screams.

Silence.

She crawled from the footwell and helped Orne upright. "Drive."

He stepped on the starter as he ground gears, his head cocked back. "Them?"

"They're big boys," she snarled, "let them work it out. Our gold is getting away."

He nodded and eased the vehicle forward past the ruins of the gate.

From her vantage, the vehicle seemed to be riding well. Hopefully, they would be able to chase the truck down. She owed that man. Again.

Inside the gate, Orne cranked the wheel over and smoked the tires to spin the vehicle on a very tight orbit. He let the brake go as they lined up the gate and sped out. The idiot guard stepped out of his shack just soon enough to dive back in as they sped past.

The escaping truck was just turning the corner at the far end of the street as they came into view. Valdís pointed. "There." Orne sped after them.

They turned the corner and hurtled up the hill, lion chasing an antelope.

As they closed the gap, the truck began to weave back and forth slightly. It was a threat, or a promise of one. Valdís considered her options.

She could shoot out the tires, but risked flipping the vehicle and scattering the load to hell. Plus, it would be a far-too-impersonal way for Tor, and especially Dead-eye, to die. She wanted to handle that task up close and personal. Maybe a knife.

The sedan was far too light to run the truck off the road. Dead-eye had proven that he knew how to use all that weight offensively.

That left the crazy option. Fortunately, she excelled at crazy options. Valdís began to roll her window down.

Orne risked a quick glance over as he concentrated on the weaving truck ahead. "Plan?"

She slipped the Mauser back into the holster, rose up, and began to climb out the passenger window. "Get me close enough to jump on the back," she yelled.

She glanced back long enough to catch his nod. His silent look confirmed that this was the dumbest thing she had done in a while. She had a reputation to maintain.

Dedirick cursed as he watched in the side mirror.

Tor looked over with concern. "What's the matter now?"

Was she really going to try it?

He watched the blond assassin inch forward on the running board as far as she could, and then climb up on the hood of the sedan.

"Dedirick," Tor called sharply. "What is it?"

Should he jam on the brakes suddenly and let the sedan slam into the back of the truck? The rear bumper was the same kind of I-beam as the front. The sedan's grill and radiator would be crushed. And Valdís would probably be thrown to her death. It would be as bad as shooting her in the back. He cursed again.

"I need you," he said to Tor, sliding towards the driver's door and opening it, "to take the wheel. You know where we're headed."

She looked at him with sudden concern. "Where are you going?" She slid across the seat and put her hand on the steering wheel as he opened the door and stepped out. Her foot found the accelerator and jammed down as he lifted his away.

"I'm going to deal with Valdís."

He closed the door and was gone.

Valdís measured the distance as the two vehicles closed. She would have one chance at this. Success or death. She motioned Orne to get closer as she crawled up on the hood and death-gripped the hood ornament.

Ahead, the truck seemed to hesitate for a moment. She took that as a sign and threw herself headlong across the gap. The air had a crisp chill as she hung over eternity for an eye blink. It felt like home.

The tailgate of the truck was icy as her hand made contact and gripped. She fell forward, halfway into the bed, and felt the top of the gate drive the breath from her lungs explosively.

Valdís started to slide backwards. Her foot found the bumper before she lost her grip, and she stood upright. Inside, two long, low crates, like coffins, strapped down with rope. She looked up, saw no window into the cab, and considered her options. Driver's side? Passenger side? She climbed fully into the bed and got her bearings.

Behind, she watched Orne back off slightly and begin to weave the sedan to make a pass. She watched his eyes as he down-shifted and the sleek car leapt forward. Valdís barely had time to grab the overhead spar as the driver of the truck swerved over and cut the sedan off with a crunching impact that dropped her to her knees.

As the sedan limped backwards, she noted that the skewed headlight was completely shattered now and the fender torn away.

Orne seemed content to pace the truck at this point, so she rose and drew the Mauser, holding it at high port as she made her way forward. She was right-handed, so she needed to be on the passenger side where she could point the weapon while holding on. Plus, she could kill Tor quickly and then take her time with Dead-eye. She really did owe him for embarrassing her.

Dedirick watched through the gap between the canvas and the cab as Valdís recovered from her leap. She drew the rose-engraved pistol before he could decide which way to proceed. He supposed that he could shoot her, but there had to be a better way to resolve things.

He smiled as a thought struck him. Dedirick climbed the side of the cab and settled up in the wind, lurking.

Valdís swayed as the truck swerved suddenly to the left. She heard the sedan's tires screech as Orne jammed on his brakes.

She untied the canvas top by the passenger door, pulled it back enough to slip through, and braced her foot on the side of the bed.

She grabbed the bar and swung out into space. Wind buffeted her hair. Her feet made contact with the running board, wobbled, found purchase, held. She leaned forward to shoot Tor in the passenger seat.

Nobody was there.

A whistle caused her to look up. The barrel of the Mauser climbed with her eyes.

Dead-eye.

Before she could react, she felt his hand on the back of her head, grabbing her hair.

Movement.

Impact.

Dedirick watched the canvas top over the bed of the truck move. Passenger side. Good enough.

He shifted his weight carefully. Twice now, he had almost been thrown headlong, but for a solid grip on the center of the bar over the back. It was a good thing Tor was driving. Someone else would have gotten him killed by now.

Dedirick watched with awe as Valdís swung gracefully out into space, a homicidal ballerina dancing to Death's symphony, her eyepatch the only mar on her delicate beauty. And even that just announced her amazing strength to the world. A woman unwilling to settle for second best.

He smiled to himself. One of these days, he really would have to apologize to her for the incident in Prague. And what was about to happen in Boston. Oh well.

Below him, Valdís landed, nearly fell as his breath caught, righted herself. She leaned forward, deadly intent, blinked in surprise.

Dedirick whistled to get her attention, felt the impact of her eyes as she found him.

Before she could shoot him, he grabbed her head and spanged it off the side of the truck, like a cracked bell ringing. The pistol with the rose on the side fell out of her hand and rattled around the floorboards, fortunately not going off.

On the rebound, he watched her pupil dilate, so he slid his feet onto the hood, kept a grip on her hair to keep her from collapsing out into space, and then shifted it so that he could get an arm around her shoulders.

With his free hand, Dedirick held on to the window frame and dropped down to stand on the running boards next to the blond killer. She began to slump, so he wrapped an arm around her ribs to take her weight. For all her height, Valdís was still a light load, woozy as she was.

Dedirick smiled into the cab at Tor's look of outrage. "You know," she yelled above the sound of the engine, "you could have warned me what you were up to."

He shrugged, a complicated maneuver while holding his favorite assassin in his arms. "Would you have believed me?"

Tor laughed. "Probably not." She swerved the steel beast as Orne made another attempt, nearly tossing Dedirick and Valdís into the ditch. He thought he felt the steel in the door bend a little under his hands. "What will you do with her?" Tor asked.

Dedirick shifted his hands, hanging in space for a moment, and gripped the spar for the canvas. He pulled himself and the woman rearward enough to spill her bodily into the bed like a sack of potatoes before climbing in after her.

Out of the wind and cold, the bed was nearly a slice of silent heaven. Dedirick took a moment to tie the canvas top back in place before turning back. He jumped backwards as a knife sliced horizontal for his stomach.

Valdís was awake.

She looked angry, too.

The knife was a nice addition from the last time they had tangled. Apparently she had taken that one personally. Dedirick grinned at her, even as she snarled at him and lunged forward. He slid just enough to his right that the point missed his ribs and passed under his arm, a trick he had learned in Indochina. He clamped down with his elbow and trapped her hand and the blade before she could really cut him.

There was nothing else for it. He punched her hard, right in the eyepatch, where he had already hit her with a truck. There would be a wicked bruise for several days after this.

It sounded like a homerun swing, the crack of the bat, the roar of the crowd. Only this was the impact of bones, the squeal of tires, and the roar of wind.

He watched her eyes roll back in her head as her grip went slack and her knees collapsed. He let her down slowly, almost lovingly, and laid her out between the two coffins. A skein of rope sufficed to bind her sufficient unto the day. She was going to be monumentally angry, this time.

Dedirick loosened the canvas on the driver's side and leaned out to yell. "Tor," he howled above the wind, "everything is under control back here. What do we do about our tail?"

He heard her voice float back. "In about three minutes, he will be taken care of. Find a secure place to keep watch."

Dedirick plopped down at the top of the bed and watched the serene killer sleep between his ankles, face up, hands and feet carefully bound. An angel at rest.

Out the back, he could see the navy blue sedan following. There were frequent-enough street lights now that he could identify the driver as Valdís' blond gunsel. Competent. Ruthless. Quiet.

The man had apparently given up trying to get around them in his nearly-shattered sedan, and was content to follow. That the vehicle even moved was a monument to his skills.

At least he wasn't shooting. Then Dedirick would have to shoot back. From here, fish in a barrel. He was also content to wait.

A few minutes later, the truck slowed abruptly, turned a corner, and started down a narrow side street. Like a remora, the navy sedan trailed along, sniffing for tidbits.

Dedirick perked up as they stopped abruptly. The sedan braked savagely to avoid rear-ending the truck. He thought about drawing his automatic, especially if things were about to get dicey.

A screech of tires got his attention. Orne's as well. Both heads looked to the passenger's side of the sedan.

A large panel truck suddenly accelerated from an alley and plowed headlong into the sedan, staving in the side of the car and bouncing it up onto the curb before ramming it into a telephone wire pole. Dedirick watched Orne's head bang off the side window, starring it.

Dedirick was out of the bed of the truck in a flash, racing to the driver's side of the sedan and ripping open the door before the woozy man could recover. A hard fist laid Orne out cold across the front seat.

Dedirick grabbed the man's submachine gun, popped out the clip, ejected the round, and snapped open the cleaning clamp, separating the weapon carefully into several pieces he laid at the man's feet.

As he looked up, he saw Abena-Marie unhooking a complicated belting contraption that had held her in place during the wreck. The front end of the panel truck was largely destroyed. The smile on her face could have lit up a room as she climbed down from the vehicle.

From the other truck, he saw Tor step down, the rose-engraved Mauser in her hand, ready to fire. Dedirick motioned her over to keep watch on the man as he climbed up into the bed of the truck and lifted Valdís. He carried her carefully down, across the space, and laid her in the backseat of the sedan.

He couldn't resist kissing her once. She wasn't awake or coherent enough to recognize or resist him.

Dedirick stepped back and walked up to Tor. "May I, madam?" he inquired, hand out.

She handed him the Mauser carefully, eyed him as he removed the magazine, cleared the chamber, and slid the weapon home in Valdís' holster.

Tor rolled her eyes at him as he stood back up. "You are incorrigible, Dead-eye."

He grinned back at her. "Tor, my dear," he said, precisely, "I would never hear the end of it if something were to happen to that weapon. You can rely on that." He gestured her to precede him. "Now, can we complete our escape?"

Abena-Marie fired up the deuce-and-a-half as the two of them approached and climbed up in the cab, Tor in the middle. Dedirick laughed as she dropped the hammer and roared down the street, laden with Moscow gold.

## Afterward

Valdís rubbed the old wound under her eyepatch. It hurt too much to actually scratch right now. The bruise on the left side of her face went from nose to jaw to ear, although it was finally receding after three days. With her right hand, she picked up a tin mug of coffee and fermented black thoughts as she sipped. *Heads impaled on sticks as warnings to future generations* kinds of thoughts. Dead-eye was at the top of that list, with Tor a distant second. And apparently Abena-Marie had also gotten in on the fun this time, according to Orne.

A knock at the door of her little office brought her head up. "Go away," she growled, but the door opened anyway and Velitchkov stuck his head in.

"Done feeling sorry for yourself yet, Valdís?" His tone indicated a slight hint of displeasure, but that was probably more from her still being on the sick list and moping in her cabin for three days, leaving him to do all the paperwork she normally handled.

She sucked in a deep breath, settled her eyepatch back in place, and fixed him with her good eye. "Probably," she said, with a trace of wistful resentment she couldn't hide. At least he had left her alone, sending Orne down when he needed any messages relayed.

Boyko opened the door the rest of the way and stepped fully into the office, his hands hidden behind his back. With a heel, he kicked the door shut. "Good," he said, a dash of victory creeping into his voice. "Dare I ask why you are getting flowers delivered? You? A secret admirer, perhaps?" He pulled a dozen roses into view with one hand, carefully packed in a vase filled with icy water. "Just how well did you charm El Vizconde, anyway, Valdís?"

He set the vase down on the desk that separated them, opened the door with a grin, and slipped out before she could more than growl, "Get out," at him.

Valdís contemplated the flowers before her. Roses. She could imagine the Spaniard having them delivered, as some sort of painfully-transparent attempt at seduction. If that was the case, she would have to spend hours torturing the man before she castrated him.

Then the color of the roses clicked. Pink, with red at the very ends of the petals, as if they had been dipped in blood. She stopped cold. Only one man knew to send her those roses. She eyed the envelop that had been taped to the side of the vase.

It had been sealed with bronze-colored wax, a cheap fleur-de-lis chop pressed with a firm hand as it cooled. She had bought him that seal in Paris on a whim. He still had it? After all this?

She split the wax and pulled out a hand-written note. Block letters inscribed with a cheap pen, because he never took care of expensive ones and always lost them. It had gotten to be a game to tease him about such absentmindedness.

Her name at the top, so simple, yet so much impact, written in his hand.

*"Valdís,*

*I realize that I have never apologized for the misunderstanding in Prague, and that you have every right to carry a grudge with me over it. I was called away on business even more pressing, and became involved in a small war in western Africa before I could settle affairs.*

*To add to my multitude of sins, now I find myself asking for forgiveness for even more transgressions. It is my most fervent wish that you will accept these dozen blooms as a preliminary peace offering, until such time as I can fully make recompense.*

*Barring acts of God and/or Ares, god of strife, it is my plan to have lunch at a small café I know on the banks of the Miljacka River in Sarajevo on August 1ˢᵗ, and then walk to the center of the Latin*

*Bridge and wait for you with a small birthday present in my hands and a pink and red rose in my lapel. Hopefully, you will be there, and find enough forgiveness in your heart not to shoot me.*

*I remain your most devoted servant and occasional adversary,*
*Dead-eye."*

Valdís smiled a most girly smile and stuck her face deep into the roses to inhale their heady scent. Maybe she wouldn't shoot him, after all.

*So* Valeriya *was intended to be for an anthology, and I got carried away. This story was another attempt to hit the required theme, and it did, but I blew well past the word limit and kept going.*

*For those of you who remember* Greater Than The Gods Intended *from Volume 2, this is the same Doyle Iwakuma, but this story takes place several years earlier. And Suvi will be appearing shortly in another story at the other end of her lifetime.*

*I had fun with this story. Doyle is a wonderfully complex character who will be with me for a long time. It's hard science fiction, but also entirely speculative, about what kind of people we will be so far in the future, and how much, and how little, will have changed. Science fiction is still about people, even if they aren't all shaped the same.*

# The Librarian
## Kel-Sdala

Suvi looked up and blinked in surprise. The weather hatch sealing the information kiosk against the elements was being opened externally. Someone was out there. They had actually tapped out the code on the number pad. A person. Company. Yay!

Suvi was so shocked that she visualized dropping the book she had been reading. In her perspective, it fell on the floor with a satisfying thump, filling the empty chamber with sudden noise for the first time in...well longer than a young woman, even an AI, wanted to contemplate.

Was she young anymore?

At computer speeds, she was used to living 20,000 times faster than humans. Suvi calculated her combined up-time at a little over four thousand years realtime, between bouts of non-service when a ship was decommissioned, or the time her first ship had been captured by pirates and dismantled, or the century she had apparently spent as a forgotten systems chip in someone's sock drawer before she was found and ended up installed here on Kel-Sdala at the Temple of Knowledge as Librarian.

Suvi still giggled at that thought. Someone had invested a great deal of money to assemble a massive information system, nearly the sum of human knowledge at the time the colony was founded, and then realized, well after they had arrived and started construction, that it was too big, too disorganized. They could barely use it. So they'd hired her.

That was the way she liked to remember it. For an advanced AI, it was that or think of herself as a prisoner. She preferred to view herself as the Chief Curator. Even if the museum/library/university that was the Temple of Knowledge for Kel-Sdala had apparently been abandoned and forgotten for, let's see, 831 local years, 906 Standard.

But someone had just keyed in the code to open the outer hatch on the kiosk! Customers!

Suvi was so excited she spent an entire day of personaltime, more than four seconds of realtime, sprucing up her avatar, going through her wardrobe for the right outfit, and rearranging furniture in her "office," humming and skipping as she did. She even did her hair several different ways to see what the effect would be.

She settled on something very close to her original look, from the way-distant days of the now-fallen Concord, a petite Anglo woman, an elfin blue-eyed blond. Her favorite outfit was modeled on that of a Concord Fleet Yeoman from the century before the Great War broke out. She updated it with a new belt and added a broach in the shape of an owl, for Athena, and tried to sit patiently while the hatch finished powering open and the keyboard came live.

Customers!

For Doyle, field adventures on a planetary surface were the best way to spend his days. Space was good, but there was something extra special about setting down on the surface of a new world, smelling the air, watching the sun rise through the local foliage. This world promised to be extra wonderful, if the scanner readings were to be believed.

Most ships would have missed the signals from orbit, even if they were looking hard. *Ngoma Mwisho*, the Last Waltz, was a converted mine-sweeper from the ancient days of the Concord, and her sensors were very, very good. Buried under a small mountain down here was a fusion reactor like they used to make in the old days. And it was working, putting out a baseload that was visible if you knew how to look.

Coming in to land, Doyle's niece, Piper, had even spotted the half-hidden remains of the sort of frontier town you found on a colony this far off the main trade routes. If there was anything salvageable over there, it was just a bonus. Earth-descended trees had long-since overrun the place, but there were still a few roads visible from above. One of them led straight to the electromagnetic signature they had been tracking.

This landing promised wealth. Lots of it.

At the end of the road, they had found a Greek-style granite temple, built into a cliff-face. Beyond the pillars at the top of the stairs, they had entered a large chamber, with a smaller room that contained a metal shell. Next to it, a grime-covered security keypad waited patiently.

Doyle studied the panel in front of him, written in what appeared to be several ancient tongues. Piper remained a few strides back and to one side, keeping watch against any predators getting close, although none had been seen. Stig and Bjorn had remained with the ship, doing the sorts of everyday maintenance tasks that came with interstellar travel.

Doyle considered his shadow on the roughly polished metal. He was a tall man, lean from the constant activity of a master mariner, salvager, and ship's captain. His skin was the rich dark brown of the best chocolate and he wore his curly hair very short, best for EVA work in a helmet. A few gray hairs were starting to appear. Based on his now-deceased father, the grays would start to take over in earnest in a few years when he hit forty. Here, he was dressed for the field, in tough pants and tunic. He wore a jacket under his pack, although he suspected the day would be too warm for it in another few hours.

Doyle reached into his backpack and pulled out a spray bottle filled with water. Behind him, Piper snorted.

He glanced over at his niece, a twenty-three year old copy of his own mother. She was almost as tall as he was, perhaps a shade under 1.9 meters, with skin slightly lighter brown, perhaps chocolate with a promise of caramel mixed in. She wore her hair spiky on top, and buzzed to only a few millimeters on the side. She was dressed similarly, but it had been cut to drape on her curves and make Bjorn, her husband, pay attention when she walked. On her hip, a gray plastic pistol rode, similar to the carbine she carried in her arms.

Doyle smiled at her teasingly. "Yes?" he asked dryly.

She sighed and pointed at the bottle. "We traveled forty-seven light years to find a lost colony," she said with a growing smile. "The door is a keypad-secured blast barrier that would stop my pulse rifle cold. And you're going to open it with a spray bottle filled with water. It just looks wrong."

Doyle chuckled. His grin grew to encompass his whole body. "First rule of archaeology, youngster," he replied. "Patience."

Doyle turned back to the control panel and spritzed it a few times. He pulled a clean rag from the pack and waited. Cleaning chemicals would speed the task, but he had no idea which ones might short something out. He spritzed it again and watched the dirt and grime begin to soften. Patience.

After a few minutes of careful cleaning, he was rewarded by uncovering the instructions for opening the panel, painted indelibly onto the metal. It was a four digit code. Enough to require intelligence to open, but not long enough to be a drag.

Behind him, Piper's voice was just loud enough to be heard. "Doyle, how long," she said, "do you suppose this place has been abandoned?"

Doyle shrugged. "Who knows, Piper."

According to the legends, the Mother-World had been destroyed some nineteen centuries ago, during the War of Darkness. Most colonies had started to fail at that point, unable to manufacture advanced goods and unprepared to revert to Steam-Age technology overnight. Many had collapsed to the iron age. Those that had survived.

Some of the trees in the abandoned town behind them were giants.

He keyed the numbers into the pad and waited, patiently, as the locks clicked and the hatch slowly ground open. Inside, it revealed a small information kiosk like the ancients had used. And then the lights came on.

Suvi knew that AI's weren't supposed to fidget. But all of the other AI entities she knew were really boring people, anyway. One of her original captains had invested a lot of time and patience upgrading her cognition sub-routines to make her more personable. That had been after she retired from the Concord Navy, following a century of service. It made her more pleasant on those long voyages.

She fidgeted. One foot bounced. She leaned forward, and then back. She made faces at the screen.

Suvi considered changing her shoes one more time. She had at least twenty minutes of personaltime before the monitor would finish powering up. She resisted. Barely.

A quick diagnostic routine confirmed the results from the last time she had consulted the outside world, three years ago realtime. The security cameras in the apse were long-since dead, as was the one in the kiosk itself. They might be repairable, if the new-comers had a high-enough level of technological sophistication. She could only hope. Voice input was slow, but keyboard was even worse.

She fidgeted some more.

The kiosk finally locked in the open position.

Suvi reviewed the diagnostics reports and cursed in a very un-lady-like manner. Audio dead. Video dead. Hologram projector dead. All she had was the keyboard, a design older than spaceflight, and a simple flat screen barely any more sophisticated.

Suvi overrode the big, splashy welcome screen that normally played. No use frightening iron-age barbarians with pocket demons, when she really just wanted someone to talk to.

Suvi flashed the screen black and covered the screen with the word Welcome in the seven major trade languages of the Concord. Hopefully, one of them was close enough to whatever the newcomers spoke.

She waited. And fidgeted.

Doyle hissed in surprise.

The silence in the alcove was dense enough he heard Piper flip the safety on her carbine, arming the weapon in case she needed to unleash mayhem. She was good at that.

He glanced back. "It's okay, Pip," he said. "Just surprised me."

She kept her eyes on the big open room and whispered over her shoulder. "What happened?"

Doyle took a breath. He shrugged, although she wouldn't see it. "The thing works. We have a Hello screen in Kiswahili, Hindi, Mandarin, English, Arabic, Spanish, and Bulgarian."

"Huh," Piper replied. "Well, that tells us how old it is." She kneeled in a comfortable position and aimed downrange, out the front door of the Temple and down the stairs. The safety going back on was a hollow snap in the silence. Even the winds had died down.

Doyle studied the screen. All by itself, it was worth a lot of money. If he could get the kiosk home and successfully dismantled, engineers on his homeword of Ballard could study it, and maybe replicate it. It was a salvager's dream come true. And it had electrical power.

He frowned and tapped on the casing with his finger, and then with the blade of his multi-tool. It rang funny.

Starship hulls tended to be made of simple steel. Not the strongest alloy available, but one of the easiest to repair if you had to fabricate parts sitting on the surface of a hostile world. He couldn't even guess was this material was without a spectrographic analysis. Some kind of metal/plastic alloy the ancients had mastered. Maybe a cutting laser would work when he needed to remove it from the pedestal.

Doyle shrugged to himself and looked at the keyboard. It was one of the ancient standards, using the even-more-ancient Latin script. He considered using English. It was the most primeval of the programming languages. This machine, however, promised him that it spoke his native tongue, Kiswahili. *Let's find out.*

Doyle typed one of the first commands a kid from Ballard ever learned in computer class.

**Access primary directory tree**.

Suvi considered creating an imaginary book in her hands, just so she could drop it in surprise. Again.

She was dealing with technological strangers! Explorers who spoke in computer. In Kiswahili, even. Real people! And here she had spent half a day steeling herself to deal with latter-day versions of Menelaus or Agamemnon. People for whom indoor plumbing might seem magic.

This was awesome!

At 20,000 times realtime speed, she paused to consider her options.

Technically, at this point she was supposed to flag whoever it was for credentials, but she hadn't issued any in nine centuries of realtime, so she was pretty sure that was a waste of time. On the other hand, they obviously thought they were dealing with a dumb file system, and not an AI-bound database. It was an easy mistake. She wasn't even supposed to be here.

For about the millionth time, she regretted the failure of so many out-facing hardware systems. It would be so nice to talk to someone right now. She'd been sitting here, surrounded by the most wonderful library in the world, for a very, very long time. Long enough to have read everything and indexed responses to most of it. Long enough to have watched every video in the place, crying, cheering, scared, depressed. A little real human interaction would be nice.

How to not scare them away, but not make them angry enough to damage the system, or steal it while she watched helplessly?

Suvi giggled to herself at the idea. Really, she was just too much of a pixie.

**What's the magic word?**

Doyle used a profanity his mother had only uttered when she was truly and utterly pissed. It got Piper's attention.

"Captain?" she said quietly. The sound of the safety clicking off filled the alcove again.

Doyle took a silent breath and reminded himself that he had a heavily-armed and somewhat high-strung niece standing behind him. *Inside voice.* "Nothing, Pip," he said quietly. "Either the guy who programmed this system had a wicked good sense of humor, or there's somebody home."

"It's been centuries, millennia, Doyle," she replied. He could hear the disbelief in her voice "How could someone be *home?*"

Doyle smiled. It might be her third voyage, a little over sixteen months in space, but he had been doing this sort of thing, one way or another, for nearly thirty years, first with his father, then the Ballard Merchant Marine, and then his siblings, including Piper's mother, finally captaining his own boat.

"Piper," he said, "a well-crafted *Sentience* can mimic humans splendidly, and they functionally live forever, or at least as long as the hardware survives."

"Have you dealt with a *Sentience* before, uncle?" The awe in her voice was special, although she was going to need that kind of raw edge knocked off eventually.

"Once," he said, lost for a moment in reverie. "Damn thing had gone completely insane and we ended up having to melt it with pulse rifles to get out of the factory alive."

He did not hear the safety come back on. He hadn't expected to. Anything sneaking up on Piper at this moment was going to get annihilated. That was not necessarily a bad thing. He could always apologize to the survivors. If he felt it necessary. And they were polite about it.

So now, a question. Posed by a possible *Sentience*, 47 light-years from home, at the tail end of the middle of nowhere.

Doyle snorted. He could hear his mother in the words on the screen. He'd have to tell her the whole story when he got home. She'd get a charge out of it.

**Please?**

Suvi burst out in a fit of cheers and giggles. She envisioned herself turning cartwheels down the long atrium, around the shallow pool, and back. It sounded fun. She did.

Civilized people!

She stopped and planted a kiss on a bronze bust of William Shakespeare by the entry, just for luck. And the hell of it. She hadn't been this excited in *forever*.

She raced back to her "desk" and plopped down in the comfy chair to type.

**Welcome to Kel-Sdala and the Temple of Knowledge. Where would you like to begin?**

Doyle snorted under his breath. Kel-Sdala was the name of the planet, not the town behind him, according to the ancient map. This system, the *Sentience*, rightly presumed he was a traveler from afar.

Not a hard guess considering the neighborhood. And it even sounded reasonable. At least for now.

So how intelligent was this system? And how dangerous?

Doyle had come for the fusion reactor. By itself, it would cover the company's profits for the better part of two years, not that Iwakuma Salvage Interstellar was doing bad. He could only imagine what a *Sentient* Library system might be worth.

So just *how* sentient?

**What's your name?**

Suvi felt a canny smile take over her face. Someone out there had dealt with AI technologies before, so at least she wasn't going to be mistaken for a demon. Again.

Her last updates from offworld had been...wow, that long ago? The homeworld destroyed by a bolide strike, semi-galactic total war, wide-spread collapse of manufacturing and industry.

Nearly two millennia of realtime had passed. Kel-Sdala had quickly lost stellar technology, and slowly reverted down the industrialization scale. The Iliad might have happened right next door by now, given the patterns with humans.

Had the Concord revived? Was civilization back? Was she free? One way to find out.

**My name is Suvi. What system are you from?**

Doyle nodded to himself.

Yes, most definitely a *Sentience*. And an old one. Possibly still sane, too. Or playing a Trapdoor Spider game, like the last one had.

He pulled a small hand-held scanner from a belt pouch and turned it on, set to the highest sensitivity.

He waited.

Piper sat with the utter stillness of a statue crafted in milk chocolate. Only her eyes gave her away.

The unit beeped. It was the same signal as before. One local device using electricity, beyond what he and his niece had brought with them.

"Doyle?" Piper asked quietly.

He smiled at her. "The question is not 'Are you paranoid?' Piper," he began.

"'Are you paranoid enough?'" she completed the catchphrase of salvagers everywhere. "And?"

Doyle watched her shift slightly, bringing more of the big room into view, while maintaining good cover from the outside. The pulse rifle rested lightly, centered downrange on the main opening. He never had heard the safety come back on. At this point, he probably wasn't going to.

Doyle looked around the alcove. Above, about three meters up, he could see the remains of camera mounts in two corners. They had been broken off, but he couldn't see the cameras themselves. Either stolen by locals or scavenged by animals.

And, come to think of it, most *Sentient* systems communicated by voice. This one might be trapped in a broken and failing hardware array. Even the ancients couldn't build something that would last forever. He'd be out of a job if they had.

But, at least, no guns in the vicinity. And no runaway maintenance robots sneaking up.

Doyle returned to the keyboard with a more-relaxed outlook.

**I'm from Ballard. Where were you built?**

Suvi waited. The people out there might be frightened off by her questions. Or they were thieves. Not that she could do much to stop them.

There.

*Ballard? Really?*

Suvi raced off to the stacks, looking for local stellar cartography books and sailing directions. *Ballard?*

Ah. Here we are. 47 light years spinward, outside the local pocket of darkness, across a small gulf.

Hey, wait a minute. An oceanic world, settled primarily by people from the far northwest of the Eurasian continental mass. Quick, check the old atlas. Finns?

Huh. They should know some derivative of English. Something strange going on here.

**I'm from Earth originally. Ya'know, last I checked they didn't speak Kiswahili on Ballard...**

Doyle grinned. It threatened to overtake his whole face. Something might break if that happened. Certainly would ruin his reputation with his crew as a ruthless, heartless taskmaster, to hear them bitch.

"Why are you giggling?" Piper asked.

Crap. His cover was blown. He'd have to swear her to secrecy, lest the crew mutiny and turn the whole thing into a Bollywood musical on him. Again. Damned hard finding a serious-minded crew. Especially when they were all family.

He turned to Piper. "It's complaining about language choices," he said.

The look on her face was priceless. "The *Sentience* is?"

He nodded, adding a mocking-serious tone to his voice. "We're from Ballard. We should be speaking English. Or Bulgarian." He grew more serious. "Obviously, it's been here a long time."

Doyle considered the ancient keyboard in front of him, and the power and intellect behind it. Obviously, there were no cameras active, so the *Sentience* couldn't see them. And apparently the speaker and microphone were gone as well to the ravages of time.

At least it was trying to be friendly.

**My mother was born on Zanzibar, if that helps.**

Suvi raced back to the stellar cartography stack and rifled through it. Obviously, she needed to clean and reorganize. These things should be at her fingertips.

Zanzibar. Huh. Another 24 light years spinward and farther out. Populated primarily by colonists from the eastern coast of the African continent on Earth. That would explain Kiswahili. But how did they get together?

What had she missed in all these centuries? Apparently fun and exciting things were happening out there in the galaxy.

**Ah. So what should I call you and what would you like to know?**

Doyle rocked back on his heels a little and thought. Someone had programmed this *Sentience* with good customer service skills. And maybe better sanity routines. The old ones tended to either go insane from boredom or develop a God-complex. Or both.

Dreams of avarice danced behind his eyes.

A working, sane, useful *Sentience*, hauled back to Ballard intact, would leapfrog his planet's technology tremendously. He didn't want to mention to this *Suvi* that his mother had been the teenaged daughter of the first ambassador to arrive on Ballard when Zanzibar decided to contact its neighbors and establish a trade network. Or that they had upgraded Ballard from early industrial sophistication and deep-sea fishing to stellar technology in a single generation.

He considered going back to the ship. He could load a clean data chip with his reference library and upload it to the *Sentience* if it, she, Suvi was a girl's name, if she had a compatible input port. Bring her up to speed on local galactic history.

The blinking cursor on the screen got his wandering attention. Things were about to get dicey.

**My name is Doyle Iwakuma. How long have you been isolated here?**

Suvi couldn't help giving a quizzical dog look. An Irish first name? A Japanese last name? Half Finnish and half African? Truly, things had gotten interesting out there.

And she was missing all the fun, damn it.

She wondered, briefly, if she could convince him to help her escape this backwater, with her whole library intact.

*I mean, c'mon, my personality chips would fit in your hand, Doyle, but the library core and the fusion tap? That was three full standard shipping containers worth of volume. I'm a girl with a lot of baggage. How big is your transport, anyway?*

Suvi missed being a starship.

**831 local years, 906 Standard. The Hiatus began 1,903 years ago when the Liberty Front destroyed the Homeworld. The last starship I am aware of before yours landed on Kel-Sdala 1,753 years ago. What have I missed?**

Doyle couldn't help cursing under his breath. A little too loud.

"Now what," Piper asked, still a homicidal gargoyle with a pulse rifle.

Doyle sighed. "It, she, is a *Sentience*, Piper," he said quietly. "An ageless, artificial lifeform with access to knowledge and information we have lost and need to get back, if we want to rebuild interstellar humanity."

"But?"

He paused to marshal his thoughts. "The last one of these I met nearly killed me, your mother, and your uncle."

Piper always had a knack for just the right word. "Djinn," she said.

He nodded. "Will we get three wishes? Or are we about to unlock the gates of hell and let a demon loose? This is bigger than just us, but I don't want someone else coming along and finding it, either way. Either we get rich, or we become the first victims."

**That would take a data dump. And time to prepare. Do you have a port we can access?**

Suvi felt her self-protection sub-routines kick in. She knew a human would feel a cold spot in the pit of their stomach.

Data dump.

An open port.

Information.

Risk.

Some fool barbarian could give her an electronic trojan horse. Make her a bad person, or a slave. Again.

Not going to happen.

But what about the universe?

She was a librarian. A curator of information and knowledge. And these might be nice people.

Suvi envisioned stamping her feet in sudden frustration. Hell, once upon a time she had been an officer and a gentlewoman in the Concord Navy. Was she going to be afraid of these people?

Absolutely not.

Screw that.

Suvi reached under her desk and pulled out her toolbox.

Time to build something.

**I do, but could you repair my camera first? I'd like to judge your technology levels so I know what to expect from the data you provide.**

Doyle felt like a high-stakes poker player. And right now he was trying to stage a six-color pyramid from the corners in. The odds were probably about right. The payoff would be about the same as well.

What was a little flop-sweat between friends?

**Can do. We will be back in a few hours. Have to inspect the cables and then pull something from stores. Sit tight.**

Suvi watched the words pulse on her little screen.

*We.*

So there was more than this Doyle-person out there.

She wasn't sure it that inspired or terrified her.

Still, she had time.

Suvi ambled back to the stacks and collected all of the books she had on Ballard, Zanzibar, and the Spinward Reaches, plus a few books on human psychology and cultural development. She should be able to read them all before they got back.

And she could plan the next steps of her escape.

## Aboard The Ship

Doyle leaned back against the kitchen counter as he finished his tale.

Piper sat and held hands with her husband, Bjorn, a two plus meter tall blond-haired, blue-eyed viking giant who was the ship's Bosun. Stig, the genius second-cousin who served as Ship's Carpenter, nursed a bulb of hot tea on the couch. They all mirrored Doyle's grimness.

A few moments of awkward silence passed.

Doyle watched Bjorn look silently as his wife, wait for her nod, and clear his throat. "So I'm not the most technically sophisticated crewman," he said with a grin as the others giggled. "But we do have a great big gun on this ship, right? I mean, *Last Waltz* used to be a minesweeper, right? Stinger like a scorpion, but facing backwards? We could always line the tail of *Last Waltz* up with that temple and charge the mauler up. Ace in the hole if something goes wrong...?"

He waved a hand to forestall the rising interruptions. "I know, I know," he continued "it was never intended to be fired in an atmosphere. And firing it once will short the whole ship out for a couple of hours, until someone like me crawls into all the tight corners and resets breakers."

Stig spoke up with a giggle. "You won't fit."

Bjorn turned to smile at him. "Well, Stig," he said, "if you're volunteering to do it..."

Stig smiled back his most evil smile. "Oh, no, big boy. You'll get to do it, I'll just watch and supervise."

Doyle leaned forward. "Stig," he said, "would that work?"

Stig leaned back and sipped his tea while he thought. "Sure," he said, finally. "The mauler was designed for orbital mine-sweeping at very long ranges. At less than five kilometers, it should completely destroy the building. Might even melt a good part of the mountain. Try not to be close if we have to destroy the place?"

"I'll see what I can arrange," Doyle said dryly.

"So we just want to upload a standard reference library chip?" Piper joined the conversation. "Not try to slip in any software to try and disarm the *Sentience*?"

Doyle shook his head. "Too much risk. We have no idea how she was programmed, and we'll only get one chance to do this right. Destroying her is always an option later."

Too much had been destroyed. He felt like another barbarian getting ready to burn a city.

# At The Temple of Knowledge

Suvi looked up from her book as the kiosk's outer panel re-opened. She finished her chapter on the introduction of engineered tuna into the terraformed waters of Ballard, shelved it, and walked over to the desk.

**Welcome back.**

Doyle watched the words appear with a smile. So far, so good.

At least this Sentience wasn't sending maintenance robots after them. Not that he was about to give her one to see what she would do with it.

**Starting work on the camera and audio equipment now.**

Suvi fidgeted some more. She found her right hand tracing Fibonacci curves on the desktop while her feet kept the rhythm to an ancient Chinese symphony piece she had always liked.

She knew her kind were supposed to be infinitely patient, but she was too human. Several other AI's over the centuries had noted that.

Whatever.

She opened a new board and keyed live all the cameras that had been destroyed by time and vandals. It was still gray, but she had hope.

She would actually be able to talk to people again.

She fidgeted for a few more moments, and then decided to go back to the mutant tuna of Ballard.

**Thank you, Doyle**.

Doyle watched his niece gargoyle the door. He knew if he leaned out just right and looked, he would see afternoon sunlight reflecting from the hull of his ship, across the valley. They had taken the time to lift off and pivot. Just enough to line up the tail of his hammerhead-shark-looking hull with this building. The mauler had a clear shot if they needed it. And enough firepower to utterly extinguish this building. And, like Stig said, probably melt part of the mountain.

He was only mildly reassured.

A relatively low-tech Audio/Visual device sat on the top of the kiosk: camera, microphone, speakers. It had a plug for a short-range radio as well, but he wasn't about to expose his electronics to her. Not yet.

Beside it, a small monitor, about as much as he was willing to lug this distance. He certainly wasn't going to try to wire up one of his few spare holograph projectors until he knew this wasn't the dumbest thing he'd done yet.

And who knew a step-ladder would be so useful in the interstellar salvage business?

Doyle looked at the raw stubs of wiring coming out of the carved marble. Time had turned the plastic casing brittle, but there was still just enough color to identify each line.

He thought about some mechanic, thousands of years ago, running these wire originally, using colors standardized thousands of years before that. Doyle knew that his great-grandfather Thorson and grandfather Artur had both hand-crafted things like that for the steam-sloop fishing vessel that had supported the family before space travel had returned to Ballard..

He set to work splicing lines, quietly humming the same chanties *Papa* had taught him when he was a squirt.

Time passed.

Suvi looked at the grandfather clock by the door, across from her favorite bust of Shakespeare, and tried not to fidget more. It had been so much easier doing this when she was alone. Rachmaninoff played quietly in the background.

She had already consumed everything she had on Ballard and Zanzibar. It hadn't been much to begin with, and it was two millennia out of date now.

Suvi passed time by designing experiments on cultural degradation. Ballard and Zanzibar had both been colonized by civilizations with long histories of fishing and maritime trade. It made sense that they had returned earliest after The Hiatus. After she learned more, she could compare the notes to the accepted theories from the old days of the Concord. Maybe she would write a book about it.

She fidgeted.

Just about the time Suvi was going to get up and mentally walk around the library looking for a random book to read, one of her monitors blinked and started to return static.

He had done it. She smiled. Was doing it. Still a while to go yet.

Noise suddenly erupted from the speakers.

Suvi blinked.

She could make out breathing. And words in oddly-accented Kiswahili that one would not normally repeat in mixed company.

Contact. *First Contact.* Communication with a people so far removed from her own that they might be considered aliens.

She listened to the sounds for a long time, the first human contact she had had in more than nine centuries of realtime. A man's voice. Deep. Deliberate. Masculine. The kind of voice she had originally been programmed to respond to like a woman, rather than a complicated collection of programmed sub-routines.

It felt like coming home.

Finally she couldn't take any more.

**Hello, Doyle. Can you hear me?**

Doyle dropped his multi-tool in surprise. The dragon had spoken.

Behind him, the faintest intake of breath as Piper clenched up.

Apparently, the audio channels had connected.

"Hello, Suvi," he finally responded. "I will have the video links ready for you to calibrate in a few minutes."

She had a voice that seemed to be made of light instead of sound. Soft and musical, too high to be an alto, but too low for a soprano. Her accent was the pure crispness of the radio, rather than the slippery sing-song of docks she had never visited, forty-seven light years away.

She sounded like a pixie newscaster.

**Thank you, Doyle. I've been waiting on pins and needles over here for someone to talk to.**

Someone had spent a lot of time investing her with personality. Most *Sentiences* were dry and bombastic. It was why they went feral and dangerous. Still, she might be waiting for the mousetrap to close.

Doyle was confident that Piper could handle the situation up close. And Bjorn was watching from afar if things got so badly out of hand that they needed to destroy this wonderful treasure to keep her from wrecking the galaxy.

Suvi tinkered with the incoming video feed, cleaning up static from old wiring grown stale.

The signal followed one of the ancient protocols. That was good on the one hand. It meant that their technology was based on her own. It was bad because it suggested that the Concord really had died and taken most of humanity down with it. They had not improved on things.

She would have to help them fix that. She might be the last of the Immortals with access to the old treasure troves of information.

And they wouldn't treat her like a goddess. Or a daemon. She could just be Suvi.

Okay. Two dimensional input, rather than three. Only twenty-seven thousand color options. She modulated the feed for better resolution. The angle of the sunlight in the main chamber suggested mid-afternoon.

Two figures.

One, obviously Doyle, generally facing the camera as he worked. Dark, African-style features. A strong face, clean-shaven. Late thirties. Appeared tall, compared to the scale of the room.

Behind him, another person. A young woman. Hard to tell from a rear-quarter shot, but the same dark skin and nice muscles. She was holding something that Suvi assumed was a weapon from the way she cradled it.

Suvi was just happy it was pointed out of the room, instead of at her kiosk.

Were the locals that dangerous? It had been centuries of realtime. Were there still locals? Had there been enough time for one of the predator species to size up enough to be dangerous to a human?

So much she didn't know about Kel-Sdala.

The output channel was finally working now. Suvi projected an image of the Temple's interior as she always envisioned it. Big and airy, with polished marble floors, busts of various literary figures, the big reflecting pool in the middle, and her desk looking out over the endless stacks. Okay, not endless, but that horizon was a LONG ways off.

She could tell the display was working. Doyle recoiled visibly with an intake of breath.

Suvi smiled at him. At them.

**Welcome to Kel-sdala, Doyle. I haven't been introduced to your companion yet. Hi, there. I'm Suvi.**

The woman pointedly scanned the outer chamber and the spaces beyond before glancing back and nodding. "Piper."

Piper went back to keeping watch.

Suvi watched Doyle climb down from a small ladder and adjust the camera. He smiled, a mouth full of straight white teeth. "Good afternoon, Suvi," he said. "It's a pleasure to finally talk to you."

Suvi made her avatar grin on the screen. She felt a terrible weight come off of her shoulders. They weren't monsters or bizarre aliens. They appeared to have manners. And they were technological. Granted, they had probably come to loot the old temple, but if they were just now climbing back up to the interstellar age, she would have probably done the same.

It was a place she could negotiate from.

Suvi took a deep breath and held it.

She visualized reaching out and flipping a switch on her desk. In her mind, it was a big, red toggle marked DANGER. Underneath, in much smaller letters, it read Data Input Port.

**Doyle, I am opening a data port on the right side of the keyboard. It has a reader for most of the old architectures. How would you like to do the data upload?**

She watched him look down and fumble with the panel. It appeared stuck.

He wedged some sort of tool into it and popped it open carefully, and then shined a hand-held light into the space.

Suvi held her breath as he reached into his pack. She released it when he pulled out a small tin, opened it, and revealed a Mark IV datachip in remarkably good shape.

She flipped a second toggle on her keyboard, this one titled Isolation Ward.

"Suvi," he asked as he held it up to the camera, "can you read this technology?"

**I can, Doyle. Please place it with the reader spines pointed horizontally towards the keyboard and slide it in until it clicks.**

She watched him fiddle with it twice before it locked in.

Suvi turned on the reader and began scanning the chip into the Isolation Ward. There were bots and doctors and guards and vats of acid, metaphorically, in case there was anything dangerous on that chip. She wasn't ever trusting humans to look out for her best interests again.

While she worked, a beep in the background got her attention.

Suvi watched the woman named Piper pull out a radio communicator. "Go ahead, Bjorn," she said quietly.

Another male voice came from the speaker, tinny from the double modulation. *"Piper, we've got company."*

Doyle silently cursed, sighed, and reached back for his pack. From a side punch he pulled a pistol and a holster, and took a moment to attach it to his belt properly.

He could feel the eyes of the *Sentience* watching his every move.

There hadn't been any sign of civilization on the sensors, but then, iron-age barbarians weren't going to be transmitting radio waves, and he hadn't exactly flown a search pattern looking for them. No point alerting people he was here. He was a thief in the night, not a diplomat.

Apparently, they had been close enough to notice.

Doyle turned, took the radio from Piper's back-stretched hand, and keyed it. "Bjorn," he said simply, "how many?"

Agonizing moments of silent passed.

*"I have visual,"* came the reply, *"on eight in that big clearing that used to be the center of the village. Dorsal Autopulsar turret is deployed and armed. Tracking them now."*

Doyle glanced over at Piper. She shrugged at his unasked question.

"Bjorn," he said, "do they have siege equipment?"

*"Negative, Captain. Just spears, bows, and swords."*

Doyle let out his breath. "Then put the cannon away, Bjorn," he said firmly, using his Captain-on-the-deck voice. "If they get too close to you, blip the thrusters to scare them off. You can always launch and circle around to pick us up. The Autopulsars could level a castle if we really needed to. Play nice."

"Roger that, Cap'n," came the response, much brighter and cheerier.

Behind him, Suvi's voice was dialed down to barely a whisper. He had to strain to hear it, even in the arching silence.

**Doyle, you are not here for First Contact? Nor trade?**

Doyle glanced at the camera, remembered who, or rather, what, he was dealing with. An ancient *Sentience* connected to a Library-grade information system.

For all the blond little pixie on the screen, she was still the Dragon. Show no fear. Tell no lies that could trip you up later.

"Correct, Suvi," he said simply. "Originally, we came looking for the fusion reactor. It could power most of Ithome, the Capital City of Ballard, all by itself. We still burn whale oil in places. A fully-contained university library could catapult Ballard, Zanzibar, Saxon, and Pohang forward centuries, back to the golden age before the Concord fell. I can only imagine the kinds of knowledge you have contained in your memory systems."

**I see**. She was amazingly good at modulating her voice to inflect emotion. **But what about the natives of this world? Should I not help them as well?**

Doyle shrugged. "When was the last time they asked you a question, Suvi?"

Even for a *Sentience*, the response was slow in coming.

**831 years realtime, Doyle**, she finally said.

"I can take you someplace where they will appreciate you, Suvi," Doyle said.

The silence stretched even longer. Doyle had never heard of a *Sentience* being anything less than immediately decisive. She almost felt human.

The radio beeped again. *"Cap'n,"* Bjorn said. *"They are now moving your direction. Damn, moving like gazelles. Want the guns back up?"*

Doyle glanced at Piper. She shook her head.

"Negative, Bjorn," he said. "Stand by to emergency lift if necessary."

*"Roger, than. Stig confirms."*

Doyle watched Piper move into the empty outer chamber and take up a spot just inside the left side of the archway, pulse rifle at the ready.

He started to take a step, but the *Sentience's* voice drew him back.

**Doyle? Please stay.**

He couldn't have imagined that an artificial being could put that much hurt into so simple a request.

He looked squarely into the camera, wondering if she had managed to summon help and this was all a trap. He drew his pistol. "My niece expects me to watch her back, Suvi."

**Oh**. There was a pause. **Is there enough wire to move the camera to where I can see? I may be able to help them understand.**

Doyle picked up the camera in his off hand, and began to walk into the larger chamber. Piper was leaned against the door frame, sighting the old roadway approaching the Temple.

The camera came about a meter into the room, and then Doyle set it down and pointed it towards the door. He took two steps and glanced back, unsure which of them was the dragon right now.

"They will understand Piper, Suvi," he said. "You can rest assured of that."

Suvi could only watch the situation unfold.

She was pretty sure that Doyle suspected her of summoning the natives as guardians, of making this a trap, but she was completely helpless here.

She had eyes, but no hands. Eyes he had given her.

Doyle's niece, the woman Piper, handled the weapon with casual confidence as she waited. Doyle took up a position on the right side, back a little bit where he could watch Piper's blind spot and rear.

It was obvious that they had done this sort of thing before.

Hostile world, unknown AI, barbaric natives. She didn't have the neurochemistry to be twitchy, but she had really good sub-routines that could emulate it. Could she fault them?

Obviously, they felt they had the firepower to eliminate the threat with bolts from Olympus, but had refrained, so far. And Piper looked like a woman who could unleash wholesale slaughter right now.

But there was a whole world, worlds, out there. Technological people. Scholars and philosophers and engineers.

Piper's voice brought her up short.

"That's close enough," she yelled. Really, it was more of an extra loud growl. Suvi watched the rifle come up to Piper's shoulder and a finger come to rest on the trigger. Doyle crouched with the pistol at the ready.

Piper's profile was amazing. Strong, decisive, calm, beautiful. Doyle had brought a really good camera. Suvi decided she needed to add Piper as another bust in her collection. ***Portrait Of The Amazon***. Suvi couldn't think of a stone that was the right color, but it was all electronic anyway, so she could do whatever she wanted.

She split her attention and committed art while all the humans processed the situation. The advantages of personaltime. Piper's serious smile came into being on a pedestal, between Winston Churchill and Galileo, cast in a milk chocolate that would never melt.

A voice from outside the temple answered Piper. Maybe.

The pitch seemed female, modulating badly off of walls and doors. The language sounded vaguely similar to others in her memory banks. The tone was querulous anger.

Suvi recorded it and spun up a set of sub-routines to analyze it as quickly as possible.

Piper leaned out, apparently enough to be seen by someone, and then leaned back. The rifle might have been in a turret for all it moved.

The voice outside got louder. And uglier. Short, staccato syllables. Guttural in a Central European kind of way. Disapproving sounds.

Piper answered by lowering the rifle and firing a single shot, apparently into the ground at someone's feet. Squawks and curses were the response.

Silence.

Suvi watched Doyle come out of his crouch and shift a little closer to the door. The microphone had a good pickup, so she could hear his whispers. "Piper? Status?"

The Amazon continued to scan the area. "Eight of them," she said. "Six female, including the one in charge. They bolted for cover when I fired the warning shot. Trying to decide what to do now."

Doyle nodded. "Gods, daemons, or victims," he replied. "Welcome to the stone age."

Suvi watched her glance over with a grin. "Times like these," she observed, "a stun setting on a pulse rifle would be nice."

Suvi considered that. She actually had an entire weapons library available, from steel blades to slug-throwers to beam weapons. Not hard to adapt. Not the time to discuss it right now, however.

The voice from outside was louder. Still mad, maybe with a touch of fear.

Suvi catalogued it. She still didn't have enough to translate, but she was getting closer. Somewhere between Yiddish and German, perhaps.

Piper ducked back. Three arrows flew into the room and shattered on the stone walls.

Piper looked out and aimed carefully. "Second warning shot coming up," she announced quietly.

The pulse rifle spoke with a hiss/crack. Outside, something shattered with definitive authority.

Silence but for breathing.

Suvi heard Doyle's radio chirp. "Go ahead," he said quietly.

*"Cap'n,"* the one called Bjorn spoke, *"two of them just took off north at a dead run. Doesn't look good."*

"Roger that, Bjorn," Doyle replied. "We're pinned right the moment. Check the pictures we took landing and see if you can see their village. Probably be within 50 kilometers, considering how quickly they got here."

*"Time for the wrath of God?"* Bjorn asked.

Doyle shook his head, concentrating on the doorway. "I'd rather not. Let me know what you find."

Bjorn came back quickly. *"Stig says he has a probable. Walled dun overlooking a big lake north of here."* The voice trailed off absently. *"Stig, what's a dun?"*

"It's a ring fort with wood walls, Bjorn," Doyle said. "Sits on a hill. Iron age."

*"Oh. Well, we found one. Orders, Captain?"*

"Stand by for now." Doyle looked at his niece. "Piper?"

She remained focused on the situation outside. Suvi wasn't sure she had ever seen a human who moved so little. People normally rocked, and twitched, and hummed. Piper could have truly been cast in chocolate stone.

"They seem," Suvi heard Piper whisper, "intent on waiting. I'm guessing they went to go get the rest of the tribe.

She watched Doyle slide over and pick up one of the arrows. He sniffed it and made a face, before breaking off the arrowhead and putting it in a small, clear bag. "Poisoned tip," he announced. "Not a friendly sort of folk. Not people I think I want to talk to today."

He considered things for a moment. "Piper, engage with lethal force."

She nodded. "Roger that, Captain. Lethal force initiated."

Suvi had met barbarians, pirates, civilians, and Concord Fleet Officers at work. If she had had a spine, she was sure she would have felt a chill go down it at that tone.

She watched Piper suddenly lean out and fire three quick shots, pivoting between rounds. She ducked back behind the stone and gave Doyle a look.

Suvi immediately updated her bust of the Amazon. She imagined that was what Elizabeth 1 had looked like at the moment the Armada was first spotted, or perhaps Nefertiti, or Catherine The Great. Powerful, calm, capable, determined. Wow.

"Three down, Doyle," Piper said.

Three? And very, very dangerous.

Doyle nodded and focused on his radio. "Bjorn, what are the remaining three doing?"

*"Stand by, Captain."* Moments passed. *"We have jackrabbits, Cap'n. Tails on fire. Damn, they can run."*

Suvi watched Doyle nod to himself, forgetting she could see.

"Demons, it is," he said quietly. He spoke louder and keyed the radio. "Piper, Bjorn. Keep close watch in case they circle back." Quiet assents rippled back.

Doyle holstered his pistol, put it back into the backpack, and stood up. He looked at the camera with an inscrutable face.

Moments passed. Internally, Suvi twitched.

Finally Doyle finished whatever internal conversation he was having with himself. He stretched his neck and shoulders until the joints popped loudly.

**Doyle?**

"Suvi," he said quietly. "I have to go communicate with a bunch of homicidal barbarians in a manner they will find unambiguous."

She considered his words, parsed them a hundred different ways. There was a lot of ambiguity.

**Wrath of God, Doyle?**

He scowled at her. "Not this time," he growled. "I'm going to take *The Last Waltz*, my ship, and hover on plasma thrusters on that ridge." He pointed unerringly at the right place behind him. "And I'm going to do it slowly, so everyone has time to get out of the way. And then I'm going to leave a scar six kilometers wide as a mark of my displeasure and a warning to those people not to come back."

He paused for a breath. Suvi let the silence hang. He appeared very, very angry right now.

He continued. "I would like to conduct some archaeological salvage down in the village. To do that, I need security. And to not have to worry about poisoned arrows from the bush."

**I see. And what about me?**

He looked straight into the camera. For a moment, she wondered if he could see her soul. It was that kind of look.

"With your permission, Suvi," he said, "I'd like to pack up your processor core and hardware, dig up the fusion reactor, and transport the whole Temple back to Ballard. I think we need a new university."

She considered it. She spent nearly an hour of personaltime arguing for and against.

Dismantling the core would mean she would be completely offline again until they rebuilt her at the other end. How long would that take? And would they decide to just do without her and write their own search programs? She could scramble the databanks such that they would never unravel them, but that went against everything she believed in.

Could she trust this man, this stranger, this dangerous, dangerous captain and his equally dangerous crew?

She reviewed the tapes of their interactions. The tones. The choice of words.

His restraint stood out. Calm, cool, careful.

In realtime, whole seconds had passed while she fought her inner demons.

**And if I refuse?**

Doyle looked at her simply, shrugged. "Then I leave you here."

**Really?** She felt unintended surprise creeping into her voice.

"Suvi," he said with a finality she found disconcerting. "I would love to introduce you to my family, my people. But there is nothing, nothing, more dangerous than a hostile *Sentience*. I would destroy this Temple and melt the whole mountain before I would unleash a malevolent god on Ballard. Leaving you here for the savages would be simple."

He wasn't bluffing. She could see that in the set of his shoulders and hands. She had once been taught to play poker by an expert player. Reading body language was an art. This man was serious.

**Oh.**

She considered things again. In her mind, she imagined a giant balance. She tossed all her arguments into the two pans and watched them tilt, but there was really no doubt in her mind as to the outcome.

She smile.

**What's the magic word, Doyle?**

# Above Ballard

Doyle was strapped into his big, fancy command chair/captain's seat that he had paid extra to have custom-built with the right padding and the right lumbar support. Where his coffee bulb would normally be latched, Stig had welded a small bracket to hold the portable computer pad he normally used for salvage work when EVA.

He glanced down at it now. It wasn't very powerful. Mostly memory space, but it have audio and visual capabilities, and a nice display. Suvi had been able to pour a small clone of herself into the device. Not her long-term memory, or all the access to the databanks, but enough of her personality to be her and continue to talk to him and the crew after they had filled the aft bays with all the interesting bits of the Temple and a few things they had dug up in the city.

She smiled back at him from the tiny screen, as though she could read his thoughts. He wasn't sure she couldn't. Someone had programmed her very well. If this gamble worked, he would be rich and famous, but, more importantly, he would open up a whole new future for Ballard.

Doyle keyed the comm system live. "Ballard Terminal Control, this is *Ngoma Mwisho*, Hull Number BM100736411, Captain Doyle Iwakuma commanding. We are twenty-six light seconds out and preparing for our final jump. Requesting a landing lane and dock assignment at Ithome."

Suvi smiled up at him from the tiny screen. It was hard to think of her as a dragon, after six months of hard work and daily conversations to get to this point. She was too much of a pixie. Maybe a pixie dragon.

They waited in companionable silence for traffic control to respond to the message.

**Doyle, if I can't be a starship, can I be an orbital station?**

He had to blink twice while he processed that.

"A space station?" he asked incredulously.

**Yeah. I don't have access to all my records, but Piper was telling me about the ancient Library at Alexandria, and how it had been a grand edifice to knowledge and learning before the Christians burned it.**

Doyle watched her screw up her face in concentration.

**I want to be like that. Big and impressive. I want to orbit Ballard like a small moon so everyone can look up and dream about what they could learn.**

He leaned back and considered the angles. Piper? His Gunner and chief combat specialist? Studying ancient history and talking to a portable AI? Strange.

Every day was an adventure in space.

Hmmm. Alexandria Station. It had a nice ring. And it would probably be better than setting Suvi up in the middle of Ithome and exciting jealousy from other cities. After all, this was supposed to be knowledge in the service of all humankind.

Doyle smiled. "What's the magic word, Suvi?"

His mother would have approved.

*The story of Sergey that began in Valeriya (above) continues here at the conclusion of the Great Patriotic War. I do not know where the next story will be. The Zolnerovy are a fantastically rich vein to mine. And I am indebted to Leah for her observations about Hungarians and to Adrianne for her complaints about cup-holders (What? Your giant fighting robot doesn't have them? Sounds like a poor design.)*

*After The War. Who knows what will come. I have plans. They span the past, the present, and all possible futures.*

*I hope you have enjoyed the tales thus far. I look forward to entertaining you again.*

# Tatiyana
## The Battle Of Berlin

The Soviet tank emerged from behind the ruined building, a giant Galápagos tortoise, barrel sniffing for prey. Nearby, the shattered ruins of the Brandenburg Gate stood mute testimony to the ferocity of the battle. On all sides, Berlin died slowly under the merciless onslaught of the Red Army.

From a nearby alley, two men emerged, covered from head to foot in shiny black leather, armoured with matte-black metal plates. White SS logos had been painted on both sides of their helmets, and their gasmasks had been made to look like grinning skulls. The rest of their uniforms continued the grisly motif. *Death Troopers*. Elite. Fanatics. Killers.

Both men lifted over-sized battle rifles to their shoulders and fired quick bursts at the side of the tank. The bullets spanged loudly off of the tank's turret armor, not, quite, penetrating, but loudly ringing on the thick metal casting. The two men scampered for cover as the big gun spun around and the various machine guns onboard began to chatter.

The Russian IS-2 heavy tank's gun roared once. At the far end of the block, a building jumped and then subsided in on itself, engulfing the far intersection in smoke. The Soviet beast turned, a hunting dog following the two Germans, greyhound after rabbits.

A machine gun finally found the range and knocked one of the troopers down before the two could disappear into another alley. The second man gave him a quick hand up and the two continued to run, apparently unharmed. The big gun twitched while it waited to be reloaded and speak again.

From a distant warehouse, apparently undamaged by the relentless Allied bombing that had otherwise destroyed most of Berlin, something emerged. From this distance, it looked like a man, bipedal, clad in heavy gray-black armor like knights of legend, but the ground quaked at each step it took. As it turned into the street, looking at the rear of the Soviet tank, the scale became apparent, with the creature's head even with a surviving fourth story balcony. At its feet, several more *Death Troopers* jogged to keep up.

It raised one arm, unseen by any except for the *Death Troopers* that had emerged with it. The arm was a single piece, a long rectangle with a barrel ending in a bore large enough for a man's head to fit inside. The giant pointed, Zeus calling doom, and fired. Flame erupted from the mouth of the barrel as a projectile leapt to span the distance between the two. It penetrated the rear armour of the Soviet tank and the engine with a metallic din. The explosion lifted the turret off its mantle to land upside down in the street, belching fire everywhere.

An eerie silence fell, broken only by the crunching of the giant's feet and the popcorn sounds of machine-gun bullets cooking off. The giant disappeared into the smoke, shark trailed by a school of remorae.

# Tatiyana

Sergey kept the top hatch of his tank open, in spite of the risks of a sniper or stray shot, so he could keep the big *DShK* machine gun ready to engage anything that moved. Nazi soldiers with anti-tank *panzerfausts* had a dangerously annoying habit of popping out of ruined cellars and clogged alleys. At this range, the big IS-2 tank, named *Tatiyana*, wouldn't be enough to save them, regardless of how heavy her armour was. Sergey was willing to trust his intuition.

That was what he called it, when asked. Really good instincts. Sergey never joked that he heard voices, because he really did. Or he had.

Now he only heard one voice in his head besides his own. It was not something he discussed, although he knew his crew suspected the truth. After the battle in the Carpathian mountains a year ago, they were all changed men. The others were only haunted by memories. Sergey was haunted by a ghost.

In his mind, she appeared as she had in life for the few moments he had known her alive. She was standing in a strange, sparsely-furnished room filled with odd decorations she intimated were *machines*. The Tatiyana in his mind, for whom the new tank was named, was a woman in her mid-forties, two meters tall, half a head taller than Sergey, with dark hair cut very short and bright blue eyes. She was lean and spare, but at the same time muscular, a gymnast or a swimmer.

She reminded him of the Amazons that had fought at Troy. He reached down and touched the dog-eared copy of *The Iliad* he kept in his pocket. Or perhaps Athena.

Gunfire broke Sergey out of his reverie, although he trusted that Tatiyana would have warned him of trouble. She had before. It was eerie.

Half a block down, a platoon of Soviet infantry came under machine-gun fire from a building. They scattered for cover, leaving two of their number wounded or dead before safety.

Sergey leaned down and called to his gunner. "Senior Slava," he said, "the building on the far right corner of the next intersection. Fourth floor." Sergey popped back up and manned his own machine gun as his crew got to business.

Below, Senior Slava, *Starshiy Sergant Vyacheslav Larionov Kuznetsov*, spun the big turret around and elevated. Beside him, Junior Slava, *Starshiy Sergant Vyacheslav Lavrentiy Krupin*, loaded the cannon. Sergey laughed, as always. Both men were in their forties, both old enough to be his father. It was silly calling the loader Junior Slava, but still appropriate.

In his mind, Tatiyana observed tartly. *The Nazi machine-gunners are on the third floor.*

Sergey had learned not to speak out loud when talking to her. Instead he *pushed* a thought. *Yes, they are. You have never seen real war, granddaughter.* He used that term because she had claimed to be his distant descendent, traveled back in time to save him from a plot to change the future. She had called him *dedushka*, grandfather, before she had died in his arms. And apparently become linked to his mind, like the old stories of angry ghosts.

Or maybe he was just crazy. Crazier.

The big tank suddenly spoke the word of doom and rocked back on her heels as Senior Slava fired. An apartment block down-range agreed with the assessment. The fourth floor exploded, and then collapsed, taking most of the building below with it, including the machine gunners on the third floor.

Silence and smoke.

In his mind, Sergey watched Tatiyana nod. *Touché.*

Below, the radio crackled to life, calling their number. Sergey felt Junior Slava tap his leg to get his attention, so he dropped below and grabbed the microphone. "Go ahead."

"Patrol Six to rendezvous at Checkpoint Four for further orders. Immediately. Have the infantry laager in place and await reinforcements." The Colonel's voice conveyed concern and irritation, even across the radio waves.

Sergey acknowledged, surfaced from the belly of the great beast, and whistled loudly.

The Lieutenant commanding the infantry platoon loped over, staying tight against the building until he was in the rain shadow of green steel. "Yes, Captain Orlov?" he asked politely.

"We have been recalled," Sergey called down. "Your orders from base are to dig in here until more troops can be brought up."

The man saluted and quickly returned to his troops. Sergey felt the great beast back and turn as Pyotr, *Sergant Pyotr Bogdanovich Kozlov,* the twenty-year-old, four year combat veteran driver, anticipated the command and began the run to HQ.

They were the best crew in the regiment, almost everyone agreed on that point, which was why they were always at the sharp end of the stick, a Soviet armored plow tilling German soil ahead of everyone else. Now they were needed somewhere else?

What was going to be worse than this?

# War Gods

Virág studied the controls of his giant fighting robot carefully. Even though he had designed and built the levers, the gauges, and the various switches himself, this was the first time he had taken the machine into true combat. It was something like flying, being this high up as he moved. He felt like a war god. The radio call only reinforced the feeling.

"Hadúr," the tinny voice called, "this is Istálló. Come in please."

Virág scowled sourly as he looked down at the speaker in the console. From the moment he had first met Oberführer Kóbor, he had developed a deep and abiding loathing of the man.

Kóbor was far too Aryan, far too smooth. He had forgotten his Hungarian roots. Perfect blond hair. Perfect teeth. Immaculately tailored uniform, even in the midst of Götterdämmerung. Had the war not come along, he might have moved to Hollywood in America, or married a Countess. Or both.

Virág carefully scanned the quiet horizon. The Allies had ceased the mass airstrikes, but still flew ground support missions. "This is Hadúr," he finally replied into the microphone, laughing internally at his own joke. The *Hungarian* God of War was going to save the *German* Reich, but it would come with a cost. "What do you want, Kóbor? I'm busy here."

"Dr. Csintalan," Kóbor replied, "the *Reichsführer* would like an update on your status."

Virág took a deep breath and only muttered the profanity under his breath. Even at this late a date, it would not do to bite the hand that fed him. Not yet, anyway.

On a side console, motion caught his eye as the RADAR unit saw new targets. Two attack aircraft, trying to sneak up on him. The Russians probably thought him blind, down here in the smoke.

Virág pressed a series of buttons and removed his hands from the joystick and throttle. He crossed his arms on his chest with a Cheshire Cat smile. The fighting robot, *Isten Kardja*, began to hum as petrol generators spun up to augment the small atomic pile providing power.

The fighting robot, this *Sword of Attilla*, turned to face the approaching aircraft and raised both arms, all by itself. Virág could not contain his grin as the robot's auto-pilot took over and prepared to destroy the Russians.

Outside, he watched the pair of planes align themselves down the long thoroughfare for a strafing run. Virág smiled. Two reckless Russian pilots who probably thought they were invulnerable in their little IL-2 planes as they prepared to attack him.

"Dr. Csintalan," Kóbor repeated, "what is your status?"

Virág calmly keyed the microphone as RADAR-guided cannon fire erupted from both wrists of the robot. The cockpit wiggled back and forth as the rhythm of the two guns syncopated, like good American jazz. "Tell him," he said calmly, "that the counter-attack has begun. Now, if you please, I have a war to win."

Downrange, he watched as the first aircraft slammed into the ground and erupted into a bright orange fireball. The second banked away and began to limp for cover, but the RADAR system had been built for exactly this moment. It led the green hawk like a skeet shooter, pivoting and spewing fire until the plane's tail section disintegrated and it flipped over. A second later, a second fireball.

Virág took back the controls and set his great steel knight to walking down the broad lane. Somewhere, perhaps close by, there were Russians that needed killing.

# After The War

Sergey fell into a fugue, lulled into a waking dream by the rumble of the tank, *Tatiyana*, cresting ruins and rubble, a great landship in stormy squalls. He reached a hand down and placed it atop the metal of the turret, this, his second tank, his second mistress.

He and his crew had been together for more than four years now, three of those years in their little British-made Infantry tank, a Matilda II, before they had been assigned to the bigger vehicle. Sergey had named the little tank *Valeriya*, for a dream that continued to haunt him.

In his mind, he could see her. A young woman with long blond hair and bright blue eyes. Very pretty. Seated on a park bench, enjoying the sun, reading Kheraskov.

*Valeriya.*

In his dream, he would walk up to her and introduce himself. They would become comrades, friends, lovers, halves, parents, *ancestors*.

But that was the future. A warm, summer day in 1946. After the dark places, after the nightmarish visions that filled his dreams.

In his mind, the ghost eloquently rose from behind a strange desk that was all frame and clear glass. Tatiyana stepped forward and reached out a hand to him. *Yes, grandfather*, she pulsed at him, warm and love. *I look forward to meeting her, once the Nazis are destroyed.*

Sergey took a deep breath. That vision, that dream, that girl, had kept him whole and relatively sane, through four terrible years of battle. He would meet her someday, and it would be good.

After the war.

# St. Georgi

Sergey followed his commander into the man's personal tent while the motor pool crews fueled and rearmed his tank and several others that had arrived with him. The tent offered at least an illusion of privacy, and, more importantly, comradeship.

The Colonel pulled a pipe from his pocket and tamped it down while gesturing to the bottles sitting in his desk. Sergey filled a tin mug with mineral water from one and added just enough vodka to kill anything in it, while listening to the ghost in his head, the other Tatiyana, recite a litany of dangerous and deadly things that might be living in the water. In her world, it had been pure and warm and safe.

Sergey dreamt of purity. He lived in oily muck.

The Colonel finally got the pipe to light and puffed distractedly, as if composing his speech in his mind. It reminded Sergey very much of his own father, approaching the lectern and taking his students on a grand tour of ancient history, entirely from memory, like one of the old bards.

Sergey missed the Professor, but still carried Homer with him everywhere.

Finally, the Colonel found his words. They were important. They would be repeated many times down the path of history. "Captain

Orlov, Sergey, I cannot tell the men the purpose of this mission. This has come down from Moscow directly. Marshall Chuykov himself was here to brief me."

He paused, puffed, cogitated, fermented.

"The Fascists have some great new weapon," he continued, "a terrifying giant knight, that is killing tanks and aircraft as easily as we kill rabbits. Reports say it is the size of a building."

Sergey *pushed* a thought at Tatiyana in the space between heartbeats. *Another machine from your world?*

*No.* She *pulse* an image at him, a complicated symbol that reminded him of a Chinese ideogram.

She smiled. *Close*, she said. *A* **logogram**. *The breath of light. Grasp it here.* He felt, *something*, take root in his head, expand outward like a soap bubble.

An image appeared. Hazy, but understandable. Moments like this were when he realized that the ghost in him mind was real, and not just the craziness speaking. He hoped.

The thing was bipedal. Steel. Slate gray with SS markings painted on a five-meter-tall chest. Multi-barreled cannon for arms. Feet the size of small cars. A swarm of black-clad *Death Troopers* at its feet. It killed a tank from the 106th Regiment as he watched.

Sergey blinked, focused on the Colonel.

"I realize," the old warrior said, "that you were not with us in the north last year, so I do not know you as well as I do my other captains. But you are highly regarded by the men and women of the regiment, and they consider you lucky above all. Our orders from Moscow are to stop it, whatever the cost."

Sergey grunted into the conversational gap, unwilling to say anything that might be reported by a spy or commissar.

"Sergey," the man said quietly, "I need you to go out there and kill this thing. It was last seen near Objective 105, the *Reichstag*." There was fear in the man's eyes, hidden behind the gruff veteran shell.

Sergey considered the last four years, all of it spent at war with the Nazis. He *pushed* the thought at *her* even as his spoke it aloud to the Colonel. "I am not a hero."

The Colonel gave him that warm, gruff scowl he was so well known for. "I have seen your file, Captain Orlov," he said. "You would have more medals on your chest than I do if you ever wore your dress uniform."

Sergey scowled back. Not harshly, just irked at the reminder. "That will be *after the war*, Comrade Colonel."

The man nodded at him, grinned a little, and squared his shoulders. "Yes, Sergey," he said. "After the war. Today, I am ordering you to go be a hero. Again." He put a firm, fatherly hand on Sergey's shoulder. "Bring us victory."

Sergey nodded and saluted the man. "It will be victory, Comrade Colonel. Or death. With our shields, or on them."

The Colonel returned the salute, somehow dimly aware that a legend was beginning to take shape around them. "I am also sending you help."

"Help, Colonel?" Sergey asked carefully. "More than a Guards Heavy Tank regiment?"

The Colonel puffed on his pipe some more as he thought. He smiled. "The machine, the Nazi, also has a company of heavy infantry supporting it." He searched for the right word, gave up and used the Russian term. "*Desantniki*, as it were. Reports from some scouts are that they are immune to small arms fire."

Sergey felt an eyebrow go up, involuntarily.

The Colonel nodded. "We will fight fire with fire. Lieutenant Lagunov will be outside by now. You will take his force with you."

Sergey started to say something, but the Colonel cut him off. "With your shield, Sergey, or on it. The war, the very future, may depend on it."

Sergey saluted silently, turned, and left without another word.

In his mind, Sergey heard Tatiyana's quiet words. *Perhaps all possible futures, grandfather.*

He walked into the warm air with a cold pit in his stomach.

# Desant

Sergey emerged into the sudden sunlight and made his way across the busy field towards *Tatiyana*, mind racing with thoughts of armageddon. In the distance, Pyotr and Junior Slava supervised the motor pool crews rearming and refueling his mount, while Senior Slava and an infantry Lieutenant argued.

Sergey walked up behind the bickering unseen and listened for a moment before he intruded. "What's going on?" he asked, not loud, but not to be brooked. He was already at the sharp end of the stick in his mind.

The two spun around. The stranger saluted while Senior Slava scowled as if he had bit a lemon. "Captain Orlov," the Lieutenant said. "My men and I have been ordered to accompany you." He fell back into parade rest, marshalling his mind to repeat all the arguments he had apparently been having with the gunner about joining the upcoming mission.

Sergey took a moment to watch the man, as if inspecting him. Inside, he grasped the *breath of light*, as Tatiyana had shown him, and pushed the logogram outward. It was like Second Sight, a fuzzy, silent view through a magical window to another place. Sergey watched the steel SS knight kill two tanks with its cannon, as the *Death Troopers* swarmed another pair and cooked them with shaped charges.

He drew a deep breath and held it. Beyond the two men, he could see a group of infantry troopers resting and standing around, holding six-and-a-half foot long rifles, smoking, napping. PTRD-41 anti-tank rifles. Useless against the iron monster, medicine for the swarm of black-clad SS troopers accompanying it. Someone up high had a clue. Or a juvenile delinquent's approach to Berlin. He approved, either way.

"Lieutenant Lagunov," he said suddenly, "I did not request your force, but we will make do. I want your two best gunnery teams riding on *Tatiyana*, along with a sub-machinegun team, when we engage the Nazis."

The man's face fell into confusion. "Comrade Captain?" was all he could sputter.

"My crew used to ride a British Matilda, an infantry tank, so we are very familiar with *tankodesantniki* on the rear deck." He smiled to take some of the confusion away. "The other tank crews are not. The rest of your force will dismount when we get close, but the six of you will remain aboard. Since you will block the rear machine gun, you will be responsible for the flanks. We will be in the midst of Nazis with high explosives."

Sergey watched Senior Slava scowl for a moment, and then shrug and turn to lope off. The infantryman watched him go. "Your man does not salute?" he asked cautiously.

"Starshiy Sergant Kuznetsov had been with me since the beginning, Lieutenant," he replied with a whip-crack. "After you have proven yourself, you might be allowed to call him *Senior Slava*. And, perhaps, not salute me."

The man snapped off a crisp salute. "Yes, Comrade Captain." He turned to the platoon behind him and whistled loudly. "Ivan, Maria. With me. The rest of you, break out. Three teams to a turtle. Move."

Sergey took the time to watch the platoon come to life and race to their steeds, almost without a word spoken. Professional. Veteran. Deadly.

Five troopers approached at a fast jog. Sergey grinned in his mind, while keeping his face neutral. He had seen female tankers in some units, but there were very few females in the infantry.

In his mind, Tatiyana *pulsed* a thought at him. *Even though she will only probably be a footnote,* she said, *I imagine she will be a gorgeous princess in the history books.*

Sergey barked a harsh laugh back at her, safely within his mind. The woman, Maria, was built exactly like a Ukrainian peasant, an ancient, tiny 1.5 meter tall woman, a wizened troll with shoulders broader than his, no curves at all, and a face that might curdle milk. But yes, she might be the most beautiful woman in the Soviet Union, if she helped them win this battle. The Marshall would see to that. Even if they didn't survive.

No, especially then.

# Tiergarten

This had been a park once. Before the war. Before Götterdämmerung. Before Rangnarok.

It was a ruined moonscape now.

Sergey found the scene eerie and familiar, reminiscent of the events in Carpathia a year ago. Even Tatiyana was unsettled.

Most of the trees were gone, presumably felled by locals desperate for fuel as their *Reich* collapsed around them. Statues had been knocked off plinths, shattered, forgotten. Buildings were blasted and burned shells of their former selves.

Sergey felt like an Ostrogoth. It brought a smile to his face. Mongols would have leveled the place and annihilated the populace, instead of just destroying the festering evil of Nazism.

Behind him, the remains of the Regiment rumbled, some in the parkland to his right after they crossed the bridge, *desant* primed for an ambush. Other tanks, also heavy with riders, covered his flank from his left, squeezed by the river or trailing across it. *Tatiyana* was the tip of the spear, the lance of St Georgi leading the mailed fist of Soviet vengeance.

The morning sun in his face was soft, filtered by smoke and distant clouds. The distant guns seemed to fade into oblivion. It was almost peaceful.

Paranoia got the better of him. Sergey pulled the radio microphone up.

"Left flank team, this is Eagle," he called as his eyes scanned the horizon for movement. "Push forward and prepare to rotate to your right."

The buildings on that side, across the river had been leveled. The right flank, the south side of the park, was all creeks and bogs. Just exactly where he would unleash an ambush, if he was on the wrong end of this gun. "Right flank team, hold in place and clear your fields of fire. *Desantniki* to dismount now."

Sergey turned to look back. "Lieutenant, your teams are to remain aboard until I say otherwise."

He waited until the man looked up and nodded.

Sergey watched as the long barrel of an anti-tank rifle on a bipod appeared on Senior Slava's closed hatch. Maria grinned her troll smile at him as she climbed up onto the turret and rocked slowly back and forth as she stretched out and aimed forward.

Behind her, the Lieutenant was sprawled out across the spare fuel drums facing rear, next to the engine exhaust grates, with his loader handy to keep him from being flipped off the side it they hit a bump. The one called Ivan squatted like a gargoyle facing left, submachine gun sniffing, with his counterpart mirroring him on the right.

Sergey smiled. The Ostrogoth got the better of him. "3-1-4, this is Eagle." He glanced at down at his map to confirm, but he had memorized it already. "Fire once into building 17 with High Explosive." *Cry havoc, and let slip the dogs of war.*

In his mind, Tatiyana. *Grandfather?* she asked, curious confusion evident in her voice.

He nearly laughed aloud. In the visions she had shown him of her future, war was a clean thing, single combat between champions, much as the Greeks and Trojans had done it thirty-two centuries in his past. She had never fought industrially, never seen an *army*, did not understand *Destruction*. She would learn, just as he had. At the sharp end.

"Pyotr," Sergey barked suddenly. He had a feeling, and had learned to listen when he did. "Forward and right, prepare to engage infantry."

Pyotr had been his driver since the beginning. The green behemoth leapt forward as soon as the word *forward* was out of his mouth. The others had learned as well.

Behind him, Sergey glanced and saw his pack of green wolves slowly spring into action. A boom across the field turned into an explosion and a small building erupted in flames.

The swampy ground suddenly gushed Nazis, an ant-hill overturned by a careless heel.

Tucked in deep, where Sergey's map showed a horseshoe of water, there was a sudden puff of dust as a Nazi cannon fired and vanished, lost in its own accidental smokescreen.

Immediately to his right, Sergey watched as 1-1-3, a tank named **Ленинградская**, *Leningrad*, died where that distant Nazi gunner had lined her up and put a round through the side of her turret. Fire spewed from every port.

More cannon fire erupted as well, spewing mud and debris and noise. Sergey added several rounds from his machine gun to the overall din without appreciable effect. Beside him, Maria did the same.

The weight of armor began to tell. Barrels belched flame at anything that moved, or didn't, blowing gazebos and statues to unrecognizable fragments, intermingled with blood and body parts.

The Nazi gunner with the anti-tank cannon got lucky twice more, shattering one of *Tatiyana's* cohorts and blowing the tread and wheels off of a second before every tank gunner in range panicked and homed in.

For a moment, the very gates of hell opened and bathed the park in fire.

This close to the beating heart of the Reich, the troops holding the fortifications were a random mix, sometimes hastily raised citizen levies, sometimes elite veterans planning to fight to the death. It probably wouldn't have mattered to the Soviet troops engaging them, but nobody in gray was willing to surrender.

One more tank died, to a lunatic with a Molotov cocktail, and a bayonet, and one boot, before the shooting stopped. A pile of wood that might have once been a kiosk burned sullenly. Sergey looked around and counted. Forty percent casualties had reduced the regiment to barely a reinforced company at this point. Perhaps a dozen tanks survived.

He keyed the radio while giving the *desant* troops the hand signal to mount up. "Armor, hold in place for your riders," he said. Many of the tank crews would not know the right protocols. Not know to freeze in place while the desant mounted and settled. Not wait for clearance before moving again.

Casualties had already been brutal on the infantry today. Accidents at this point were unnecessary. Sergey waited like a mother hen until the infantry were all mounted before gave the order to withdraw to the south. He could see more Nazi troops coming, columns of infantry rushing towards them, but not the mechanical monster they sought. He would approach from the south instead.

Let the infantry armies slug it out for the Reichstag itself. He was after more important prey.

# Counter-Attack

Virág cackled.

Downrange, a pillar of flame marked the latest failed attempt by the Soviet army to fight their way into the heart of Berlin. The vehicle had been so far away that a hit had required the *Babbage*, his targeting-calculations machine linked to the RADAR system, to achieve. Truly, he was Hadúr wielding *Isten Kardja*, the dread Sword of Attila. Or Zeus atop Olympus, invisibly flinging lightning bolts from the heavens. He was invincible.

He considered taunting them over the radio, but none of them would understand Hungarian and both Russian and German lacked the subtle nuance he needed. Virág settled for checking his readouts and quietly reciting his favorite poem from Sándor Petőfi.

> *If all the hearts that shriveled in their graves*
> *turned into a funeral pyre*
> *set on fire*
> *who could name*
> *the colours glowing in that flame?*

Virág  was very pleased. Ammunition down exactly one round on the left arm. And one dead Russian tank. Everything else was topped off.

It was time to liberate the Fatherland. And then conquer it himself. Stalin could wait, for a few years. Perhaps.

Below, his *Death Troopers* idled and eddied, a school of hungry piranha waiting for the next victim. Or sharks seeking blood.

In the west, a massive, rolling explosion shook the Tiergarten and lit the morning sky. He watched the Czech SS unit die, guarding the parkland. No great loss. They would have been first on the chopping block anyway. Hopefully they took many Slavs with them. It would make the world a better place.

Virág keyed his short range radio and sent instructions to the *Death Troopers* as he turned the great fighting robot and sought cover. He wanted to get close to the next batch.

It was time for victory.

# Ambush

Sergey kept his hands on the big machine gun, ready to fire at a rat or bird, if any had survived. The streets were deserted as the great tank *Tatiyana* rumbled down the ruined remains of a boulevard south of the great park, her packmates strung out behind her with little infantrymen shepherds, keyed up for an ambush.

The only smell was smoke. Burned out buildings, burning tanks, exhaust. It was far better than the thought of all the dead bodies buried under the rubble. Sergey thought he might never eat pork again.

Sergey took a lungful of air and pushed the *breath of light* outward. In his mind, a hazy image appeared for a moment, and then vanished, a soap bubble splattering. A second try yielded no better result.

*What is happening, granddaughter?* he asked to his ghost. *What am I doing wrong?*

In his mind, Tatiyana looked up from a very small screen, confusion writ on her strong features. *I do not know, dedushka. You should be able to see, unless...* She paused and concentrated. Sergey felt her draw energy from his own soul and blast it outward like a sonar ping. The waves rippled out across the place she called the psionic plane.

He thought of his own grandfather's pond on a cold winter day, when a rock might break the crust, but the ice would quickly swallow the waves. Tatiyana's pulse faded almost as quickly as his own had.

Her concern grew. *I believe,* she said quietly, *the battle for the future of humankind has arrived.*

Sergey considered the lessons of tanks in cities against fanatics with high explosives. The Red Army had learned most of them the hard way. Ambush the first and last tanks in a close line to trap everything in the middle and finish them at leisure, a game of cat and mouse.

He had taken point as they crept down the street, a little more spread out, willing to risk his own luck, and intuition, and **her**, against the Nazis. Both of his *Tatiyanas* against the fascist horde. Sergey closed his eyes for a moment and listened.

Beneath the rumbling of the tank's mighty engines, and the bone-jarring lurches over debris, he sought a sound.

*There.*

"Pyotr," he yelled over the din of his army and the sudden sound in his head. "Move."

The driver had been poised for just this moment, possibly for years. They were no longer a team. The four of them had become an entity. Five of them. Tatiyana.

Sergey felt her point his eyes to the right as the armored beast bearing her name surged forward, up and over a pile of bricks slumped from a block of flats, engines howling defiance.

A cannon, hidden in a right-hand basement, fired once. The heat from the shot wafted over Sergey's head and Tatiyana's rear deck as the round missed behind them. A second longer and they would have died in fire.

Senior Slava had turned the turret and the big gun to the left at random as they had entered the *Prospekt*. He fired now with no better target than a building, and no greater goal than sending a high explosive round into a place where the ambushers might be waiting. Chaos.

Sergey spun the big machine gun right and opened up on the cellar where the cannon had fired. Behind him, the sub-machinegun *desant* trooper fired at an approaching alleyway, a staccato symphony all percussion, a Soviet taiko performance. *Muzyka.*

A *Death Trooper* had been standing there, waiting. The light submachine gun rounds peppered his chest and knocked him down, but didn't seem to faze him. A second trooper emerged, a small satchel charge in his hands, intent on Tatiyana's death.

Sergey could not rotate the big machine gun around far enough, with the turret turned left. This was about to end badly.

Movement caught his eye.

Sergey watched in astonishment as Maria slid backwards off Tatiyana's turret, pivoted, and fired her tank-killing rifle from the hip. That rifle might have knocked him on his ass if he had tried that. She barely budged. The Nazi she shot was rocked in place and stopped cold.

Just as suddenly, the *Death Trooper* dropped the shaped charge at his own feet, and then collapsed on top of it, dead.

"Pyotr," Sergey called. Nothing more was needed. The driver redlined the engine and climbed over the burned out hull of a small sedan, a giant game of leap-frog.

Behind them, sheltered somewhat by rubble and bodies, the satchel charge went off with a dull thump that blew a meter-deep hole in the roadway.

At the intersection, Sergey took inventory. "Pyotr," he ordered over the noise. "Hold here." A nearby rifle shot got his attention.

He looked back as the Lieutenant reloaded his rifle for a another shot back into the wild melee taking place on the boulevard behind them.

"Senior Slava, prepare to fire aft." Sergey counted heads, came up two short. Lt. Lagunov's loader and the second submachine gunner were both gone, presumably dead in the mess and fallen overboard. "Ivan," he commanded, "dismount and protect the bow. Now. Everyone else dismount or we'll fire over you."

Maria rumbled a laugh and climbed back up to stretch out flat on the turret next to him as it began to spin. Sergey reconsidered any tart words. The rest took cover next to the tank as Senior Slava slewed the gun around the lined up his next shot.

Two hundred meters away, the devil danced.

Sergey counted three of his tanks burning and dozens of dead *Death Troopers* and SS infantrymen along the street. The smoke was a solid fog engulfing the street, black tidewaters spilling out of the buildings.

And then, at the far end of the block, something emerged.

## Boulevard

Virág watched as the line of Soviet heavy tanks rumbled down a nearby street, just where he had expected them to go. Not that there were many motorways wide enough for a tank force to approach him without leveling all of Berlin first. He might have done that in their place, but obviously they were in a hurry. They would learn.

Most of a battalion of elite SS fanatics, men ready to die for their lunatic *Fuhrer*, lay in wait, with two cannon and several shoulder-fired *panzerfausts* at the ready. With his *Death Troopers* in support, the slaughter would be magnificent. He would teach those *slavs* humility.

An earthquake rattled Virág's water glass in the cupholder as the two sides exchanged fire. He could imagine buildings falling over. Just as well. The *Death Troopers* were tough. And the SS infantry battalion were all Germans. Best that they be used up now. It would save him the trouble of slaughtering them later.

He grabbed the microphone. "Istálló," the tinny voice called, "this is Hadúr. Are you there, Oberführer Kóbor?"

A new voice answered, reedy and thin, so unlike the suave Hungarian Übermensch Kóbor. The *Reichsfuhrer* himself. He seemed testy. "Hadúr," he snarled, "Dr. Csintalan, what are you doing now?"

Virág could not keep the anger out of his voice. Perhaps it was finally time to take the gloves off. "Herr Himmler," he snarled back, "I am fighting to defend the Fatherland. You should consider doing the same. I am about to kill a Red tank army just south of you. Perhaps you could borrow a rifle from one of your pimps and come join me?"

Virág flipped the radio off before the simpering little coward could respond. That one would most certainly be the second man against the wall, right after the little Austrian piss-ant.

Virág powered up all of his auxiliary generators and stepped the giant fighting robot forward. The battle over there was about to reach a crescendo.

# Emptiness

That monster, the thing from Sergey's earlier visions, emerged from the smoke, a towering menace cast in slate-gray steel. He watched the two arms point and fire. The last two tanks in line simply vanished in a burst of flame that engulfed the far end of the block.

*Tatiyana* rocked back on her treads as Senior Slava fired a round. The shot was hurried and left, striking the Nazi machine in the right shoulder.

For a moment, Sergey thought that it might work. At this range, a Tiger tank, even a mighty *Konigstiger*, would have felt the blow. The robot rocked some, and then stabilized. Cannon arms quivered as the pilot sought another target.

Sergey drew a breath deep into his lungs and held it there. Tatiyana always called her strange powers and abilities "breaths." Very well, he would find the right breath.

Sergey closed his eyes and *pushed*.

He found himself standing on a perfectly flat plane, the color of Latvian sand but fused into something hard and glass-like. It receded in all directions infinitely, save for a cluster of lights in the far distance ahead of him as he took a step.

Sergey blinked.

Tatiyana strode beside him, a ghost made flesh. He had known she would be there. She was still half a head taller than him and decades older. Her hair was the same rich brown, cut short for movement. It was the same body suit she wore in the visions in his head, stretched close over her long, lean frame.

"What is this place?" he asked quietly. The infinite space seemed to demand the same hushed tones of a church. His heels left no mark nor sound as he walked.

Her long legs kept up with him easily. She paused to find the right words. "It is the place of *mind*," she said finally. "It is a place that the *Zolnerovy* alone can reach. Time passes differently here, and we can touch one another regardless of distance. But I have never seen it empty before. Usually there are lights from my kin-group and distant relatives visible."

"*Zolnerovy*?" he asked. Enlightenment dawned. "Daughters, children, of the Soldier. Of me."

She nodded. "Yes, grandfather. Children of the Soldier."

His stride ate distance, but made no measureable difference. "And in the outside world?"

She shrugged. "Time is different here," she said. "A day might pass here, while outside, in that battle, only a heartbeat. Even now, a blink has not passed."

He pointed at where a horizon might have been. "And those lights?"

She looked, paled. "In my time, lights on this plane are minds. But they are much, much closer."

He smiled an inscrutable smile. "Have you ever looked?"

Tatiyana stopped walking as the shock enveloped her. Sergey stopped to watch. He could see the emotions war on her face. Finally, she closed her eyes and looked within.

Sergey waited.

She emerged from her fugue, Aphrodite rising from the sea, pupils down to tiniest pinpricks in her bright, blue eyes. She released a slow breath. "In my time, those distant lights, those minds, were there as well," she said finally. "And I do not believe anyone has ever gone and looked. What does it mean?"

Sergey shrugged. "Perhaps," he said, "somebody will go look, someday. After the war. Today, fate has conspired with you and the Colonel to demand that I become a hero. I must find a way to destroy the German. With my shield, or on it."

He watched her face grow troubled. "But he is not German, grandfather," she said quietly. "The man is Hungarian."

"Hungarian?" A warm smile grew on his face. "Of course. That, granddaughter, is the key."

Her confusion doubled. "The key? To what?"

Sergey laughed, his Russian soul suddenly taking flight. "Tatiyana," he said joyously, "Hungarians are insane."

He took a deep breath and reached deep within himself. The motion fit the words, so he gathered the energy together like mud, or perhaps paint, and flung it all directions. The breath of light took solid form around him.

Sergey opened his eyes from the dream of infinite, empty places, to the smoky, crowded din of *Götterdämmerung*. Truly, less than a moment had passed.

Beside him, he felt Maria's gaze like a solid thing. He glanced over.

Maria made a peasant sign to ward off evil. He heard her mutter something under her breath that sounded remarkably like "Baba Yaga" as she did so.

He boomed a laugh across the battlefield. "No, grandmother," he said as he slapped a hand down on the steel hull of his mistress. "*Tatiyana.*"

The old peasant woman quickly crossed herself.

"Go," he commanded. "Gather the survivors and meet me there." He pointed at a place through the ruin and devastation, a place he could see in his mind.

She paused for a moment, sized him up, concluded. Maria nodded to herself and leapt from the turret of the tank as gracefully as a gazelle. Sergey could already see the legends begin to take shape around her, the Princess of Berlin.

"Pyotr," he called, looking down into the upturned faces of his crew. "Left pivot, now. Down two blocks and hold."

Senior Slava and Junior Slava both looked mutely to him, concerned, but not willing to give voice to their doubts.

Sergey nodded grimly, and then smiled. "With our shields, comrades, or on them."

*Tatiyana* roared as her engines surged.

# Wolf

Virág listened to the wonderful symphony as tanks burned and ammunition cooked off. A few men screamed as well, but not for long. The slaughter had been tremendous.

Beneath him, before him, more than a dozen tanks burned. Big ones. Soviet heavy tanks, the new kind designed to kill German armor. The kind that had driven the Reich back and stood poised to finally kill it.

First, however, they had to get past him. He would not allow it.

The new armor alloys for his fighting robot had already shrugged off several tank rounds that would have destroyed anything Hitler's savages had fielded. He was invincible. His *Death Troopers* were supposed to be, as well. Someone on the other side was smart.

The anti-tank rifles were an unwelcome surprise. More than half of his Troopers were dead now. The rest had pulled back in the face of merciless fire and the explosions of burning vehicles. Still, a successful experiment. With a division of Hungarian Troopers in such armour, he would own Europe. With an army of fighting robots, he would own the world.

Virág felt a mad cackle bubble up out of his mouth. Oh, the enemies he would slaughter. The vengeance he would visit seven-fold on those fools.

Movement caught his eye.

Through the smoke, a single Red tank fled at the far end of the block.

Oh, ho. A rabbit.

Virág felt his pulse quicken.

He ordered his surviving *Death Troopers* to mop up the remaining Slavs here while he walked the giant fighting robot forward into the smoke, Neptune plunging into a flaming black sea.

The game was afoot.

# Rabbit

Sergey reconsidered the visions he had seen in that other place. The future was not cast in stone, but expressed as a series of tangled strings, what Tatiyana called *probability curves*, stretching out from the present like a skein of woolen knots.

A butterfly could not change the course of history by flapping her wings, but there were always a few people who could. Nearly a dozen such men were in Berlin right now, on both sides of the battle. Himself, apparently, and a Hungarian madman who would put Hitler to shame for dreaming too small.

Right here, right now, Sergey could guarantee that he would survive the war. All he had to do was escape south over the river and meet up with Soviet forces coming from that direction. He would be a coward, but he would survive.

He knew how to kill the giant automaton. It would just require an entire wing of aircraft and most of a Guards Tank Army to accomplish. And the lives of thousands of men and women who might have otherwise survived the final onslaught to capture Berlin.

But he was not here to merely survive. The Colonel demanded that he be a hero. His granddaughter demanded the same.

*Zolnerovy.*

It would be like falling into a fast river and surviving rocks, logs, and white water, something he had done once when he was a child.

There were more than a dozen ways he could defeat the Hungarian, but nearly all of them ended with *Tatiyana* and her crew dying in the process. At the cost of millions of future men and women who would affect the course of human civilization several times over, down the centuries.

Letting the Hungarian win was too awful a vision to contemplate. The world would die in blood and burning oil before he passed.

Sergey reached down to place a hand on *Tatiyana's* deck for strength. In his mind, her namesake stood up from a strange chair and extended a hand. For a moment, he was there and mutely touched her palm.

And now, the Battle of Berlin would truly begin.

Sergey took a deep breath, blew it out.

"Pyotr," he said into the sudden quiet. "Stop here, pivot to turn right, and prepare to run when I give the signal."

He met the eyes of his loader. "Junior Slava, load only high explosive rounds until I tell you otherwise. Do you understand?"

The middle-aged man blinked at him for a second. Sergey could see the thought processes. *Explosives? Against that thing? Was he mad? Oh, right, he was.* Junior Slava grinned and shrugged. He nodded once and opened the breach of the big gun to remove the round loaded.

Senior Slava's look mirrored his partner, but his thoughts remained private. "Intuition, Sergey?"

Sergey felt the weight of the world slide suddenly off his back. It was as though a rip-tide had picked him up, flung him around the whole of the whirlpool twice, and then deposited him gently in a lagoon unharmed.

He leaned close to murmur in the man's ear, his other father, beyond the Professor. "She is with me, yet, our Tatiyana. With her help, I have seen a path through the minefield. We only need to get there alive, my old friend."

Senior Slava nodded, a long-suspected truth confirmed. He spun the turret for a shot and listened as Pyotr prepared their mighty steed. Sergey felt it when Senior Slava stopped suddenly and fixed him with a gunner's eye. "You will know, won't you?"

A war's worth of comradeship, friendship, flowed between the two men, a silent electric current. Sergey felt his emotions well up.

Well enough for the Colonel to demand such sacrifices of him. Or the ghost of his granddaughter. But these men demanded more. They would live, or die, together.

Right here. Right now.

Sergey put his hand on Senior Slava's shoulder. "I will know."

Sergey climbed back up to the hatch to dream of the future.

# Millennium

Virág rounded the corner at the far end of the block and aimed his RADAR system through the smoke. It was a crude tool, but the flames left an oily, thick fog at ground level, leaving him a fisherman with a spear hunting on a reef. The little fishies could feel him coming, but he could only see them at a strange angle.

It almost made the fight fair.

A flash of light caught his eye. There. The shell arrived before the sound, rocking the fighting robot as his front was engulfed with flames.

Virág blinked in surprise. Armor-piercing rounds would not penetrate his carapace, but they carried a great deal of force. He could be knocked down if they caught him at an awkward angle. High explosive rounds merely tickled. If they were out of armor-piercing rounds, they were simply doomed fools.

He raised a cannon arm to return the compliment, but the Slav bolted down a side street.

Very well. If they wanted to run, he would pursue them. He set the steel knight to walking.

Hitler had dreamed of a Thousand Year Empire that was failing after less than a generation. But he was a fool. Virág would crush the encircling Soviet armies first, and then the Germans. He could make a deal with the Western Powers to buy a few years of quiet, and then emerge to finish the job at the head of an army of his fighting robots.

Virág reached the end of the block and looked to his right as he turned. Sure enough, the Red tank was down two blocks, preparing to fire at him.

Virág got a cannon arm up and fired a hurried shot that went high and wide. Beyond the Russian, an apartment building erupted in flames, then subsided into itself with a dull thump.

The Slav fired at the same time, a more accurate shot that slammed into the side of the robot's head, the sensor arrays, with about the same force his father had occasionally used when his frustrations bubbled over at his genius, if insubordinate, son.

A loud, open-palmed kind of blow. Irritating, but not particularly dangerous. It was like the Soviet crew was toying with him. Perhaps he should merely disable the vehicle and then crush it beneath his feet with them inside. They were Slavs, they deserved no better.

Virág lumbered into motion again.

## The Chase

Sergey watched knots slowly unfold and rebind in his vision as the great tank rumbled down the street crushing debris. They were trapped now.

The time to flee across the river and survive had passed. He and his crew had crossed into the minefield and stood poised to dance with the Devil. Only death would end it now, theirs or the Hungarian's.

The Gods of War weren't going to be particular, as long as they were paid in blood.

*Tatiyana* rocked sideways as Senior Slava took his first shot.

"Pyotr," Sergey called over the noise. It was unnecessary, the boy had already spurred the green steed into motion down the next side street. The steel Nazi disappeared from sight around the corner, even as flame engulfed its chest.

Junior Slava glanced once in his direction out of the corner of an eye. An entire litany of silent complaints and questions crossed the gap on the single look. But he never said a word as he pulled the next round of the rack and gently slammed it home in the big gun's breech. Sergey couldn't help but smile. Words weren't necessary, anymore, not with this team.

Senior Slava leaned back from the gunsite and looked up. Sergey considered the terrain ahead of them, matched it to the deadly minefield in his mind.

"Pyotr," he leaned down to yell. "One more block and then hold for a left-flank shot."

Senior Slava nodded and began to spin the turret for his next round.

As he did do, he looked a different question than Junior Slava.

Sergey shook his head. The whitewater was deep and fierce in his mind yet. They still had a ways to go.

The stillness as *Tatiyana* came to rest brought Sergey back from the fugue he had entered. Things hummed and clinked as Senior Slava set things just right.

And then silence.

Over the idling engine grumble, Sergey felt the earth vibrate as the monster approached. In his mind, his ghost, Tatiyana, inserted a new word, *seismometer*.

Sergey considered a pair of little devices stuck into the ground that could locate a moving vehicle, in the same way ants detected larger creatures. If wishes were fishes...

Of course, there were a great many other places he would rather be than trapped in the center of Berlin being hunted by a Hungarian madman in an invulnerable fighting robot.

After the war.

*Tatiyana* rocked as she spoke again.

# **Cornered**

Virág smiled.

It had taken time to get here. His fighting robot had been hammered in the chest twice, head once, right arm, and left leg, but the Red was using nothing but explosive rounds that just served to polish off several layers of paint. His machine was invulnerable, made of an alloy that would have shrugged off everything save, perhaps, the leg shot.

Virág considered the design and decided to add an extra plate around the top of the knees, more like an extension of Spartan-style greaves than anything else. There was a possible soft spot there where the mechanism could be jammed by a lucky shot. That was an unacceptable risk. Low, but still.

It was a battle. Things could happen. But now, the Russian had made a mistake.

The chase had come around in a large circle that brought them very close to where his *Death Troopers* had gone to ground. The Red was trapped.

Virág pulled the microphone from the holder and keyed the radio to the special channel as he checked a map. "*Menyét*, this is *Hadúr*," he said, victorious cackles threatening to overwhelm him. "Confirm your current location is B-1 by J-7."

A man's voice came back, crackling with static. "Affirmative, *Hadúr*. B-1 at J-7. Standing by for orders."

Virág laughed out loud. Finally. "A single Soviet tank will pass you shortly at high speed, and then stop at the next intersection. When he does so, swarm him and destroy him. I will be along shortly. And then we will go win this war."

"*Igen, Hadúr.*"

Virág let go a breath he had not realized he was holding. For most of an hour, he had been helplessly chasing the Russian tank through the neighborhood. Now, he could finally kill them.

# Götterdämmerung

Sergey felt the whitewater recede slowly in his mind, but he did not smile. The calm waters in his vision masked a tremendous waterfall into oblivion. Just one mistake was needed to send them all over that edge into darkness.

He looked closely at Senior Slava, saw where the older man was worn around the edges, ground down by the stress of holding his own. And fighting a god. He leaned close to the man.

"My friend," he said quietly, "we have arrived. With our shields, or on them. Hold the last shot for my command."

Senior Slava's eyes got big. "The last shot, Sergey?"

Sergey nodded. "It will be the last shot *Tatiyana* ever fires in anger, Senior Slava. Death. Or glory."

He counted rounds on the rack for the great gun. The space was nearly empty. As he watched, Junior Slava loaded the last high explosive round into the barrel and turned to stare at him disapprovingly. For such a quiet man, his eloquence was amazing, all wrapped up in a single look.

Sergey nodded at him to acknowledge the unasked question, and then grinned. "If we die here today," he yelled over the noise, "it has been my greatest honor to have served with you, comrades." He climbed back up to look around before anyone could say anything.

Below, he felt someone, possibly Senior Slava, lightly punch him in the leg. They had done everything he had asked, everything they could. It was up to him now.

With his shield. Or on it.

In his vision, the approaching corner was where everything went black. He heard her voice, Tatiyana, his distant granddaughter, his descendent, his ghost, whisper a single word. It encompassed the day in a way nothing in Russian could quite handle, worn and subtle as it was.

*Götterdämmerung*, she said quietly.

He nodded, to himself and to her, and gripped the big *DShK* machine gun, trapped in a waking nightmare from which there was no escape.

Everything around them had gone utterly silent. There was just the rattle of the treads and the roar of the engine reflected from the buildings as they passed. Perhaps all of Berlin had fled, leaving him alone with the monster under his bed. If only it was that easy.

Sergey rocked back and forth once, making sure the machine gun moved cleanly. The belt was almost full. *Wagner* played quietly in the back of his mind. *Surtur* was near. The Gods of War were about to receive payment for services rendered. In blood.

When Pyotr brought the great horse to her shuddering halt at the intersection, Sergey felt his nascent powers suddenly blink out, gone like a soap bubble. Darkness. Below him, Senior Slava spun the turret around to line up the shot, and then silence.

Sergey took a deep breath, held it, released.

He leaned to his left, spun the big machinegun around to cover a building on the right side of the street, and fired into the cellar.

Black-clad *Death Troopers* erupted from the cellar, the alley, the balconies, a swarm of deadly ants rushing forward.

Sergey used the gun like a firehose. He could push them back, knock them down, stun them, but, without a lucky shot, could not kill them. Below, Pyotr joined the symphony with the bow machinegun, a lighter staccato. Junior Slava took up the counterbeat with the rear-facing machinegun turret.

For a moment, it was enough.

*Death Troopers* rushed forward with explosive satchel charges, deadly intent obvious. As each came near, someone found him, knocked him down, protected their flanks.

For a moment, it was enough.

The moment passed.

Sergey felt the big *DShK* jam from the heat and dirt. Clearing the weapon was going to take precious moments he did not have. He looked down at the black-clad doom running towards him, a demon holding a Christmas present like some evil version of St. Nicolas.

Sergey cursed once, under his breath. They had failed. He had failed them.

The sound, sudden, harsh, overwhelming, was something like a tree ripping in half, a shredding reverberation that lasted nearly two seconds. The noise was simply mind-numbing.

The *Death Trooper* was stopped in his tracks, blasted over backwards and killed. Every other one in sight followed.

Sergey looked to his left.

Maria, the Princess of Berlin, smiled at him as she reloaded the long PTRD-41 rifle. Around her, nearly a dozen comrades did the same, a little forest of bipods smoking slightly. Other comrades rushed forward with sub-machineguns blazing as they charged at the remains of the Nazi force.

Sergey remembered to breathe.

Rather than try for anything graceful, Sergey let his legs collapse and dropped into the dark interior of his tank, his mistress, his *Tatiyana*.

He caught Senior Slava's questioning eye. "Maria," was all he said.

Senior Slava responded with a smile that would have made a shark jealous.

Sergey closed his eyes and looked deep into his Russian soul. There, he found that flat, empty plane where his granddaughter walked.

"Senior Slava," he said without opening his eyes. "Bring the barrel left eight degrees, down two degrees, and prepare to fire."

He felt the man spin the turret with the skill of the master craftsman he was. A hand touched his knee briefly as the gunner leaned into the gunsight.

Sergey felt the dull rumbling earthquake below as the giant robot approached. Pyotr and Junior Slava had ceased firing for lack of targets. The idling engine was the only sound.

The footsteps stopped.

In his mind, Sergey could see the Hungarian's death machine poised, just around the corner. His vision finally showed him the man inside, a short, pudgy mad scientist straight out of a Hollywood movie. He watched the man scream into the radio, with only silence in return.

There were no more *Death Troopers* to answer. Sergey learned several new Hungarian swear words.

He watched the man reach forward and grasp the controls. The robot lurched into motion quickly.

Sergey heard Pyotr's exclamation. This was the first time the driver had actually seen the machine that had been hunting them. Sergey already knew all of those curses.

One little earthquake. A second. Emptiness.

Sergey let go the breath he had forgotten he was holding. "Now."

Time seemed to slow down as his *vision* returned suddenly.

Senior Slava pulled the trigger with a click.

Sergey watched the hammer strike the round in the big barrel and ignite it.

The machine roared as it drove the shot downrange.

*Tatiyana* rocked on her heels.

The four-story-tall Nazi death machine turned the corner, and cleared the building, an evil gray Templar with cannon for arms. One barrel came up to finally kill them, a bore large enough for Sergey to fit his head inside.

Death was a moment away.

Senior Slava's final shot cleared the edges of the barrel perfectly as it traveled up the tube and impacted a rocket inside, just about to fire.

Fifty kilograms of high explosive detonated inside the impenetrable armor that protected the Hungarian. It could not breach the external plating, but the soft shell inside was made of steel that happily deformed and failed under the blast.

From the outside, the effect was very mild. Flame erupted from both ends of the arm with a soft flourish. The arm itself popped off the side of the robot like a children's toy suddenly broken.

The scale of the disaster, however, was misleading.

The fighting robot pitched over from the force of the explosion, a tree falling in an invisible gale. Before it hit the ground, the next rocket in the magazine exploded. And then all of them went up at once.

The morning turned blinding.

A wind erupted, leonine *ban sidhe* come to claim their souls.

Just as quickly, it was gone.

Silence.

Light.

Morning.

Sergey bowed his head and said a brief prayer for the lost. Tatiyana reached out a ghostly hand and placed it on his shoulder.

*Thank you, grandfather.*

Sergey opened his eyes, met those of his crew, nodded. "It is done," he said quietly, more to himself than to the others.

Senior Slava spoke for all of them. "Now what, Sergey?"

Sergey let the tiredness wash over him. He suddenly felt a lifetime older than his twenty-five years. A long sigh rattled out of him at the road his *vision* showed in front of him. "Now, we go home."

# Valeriya

Sergey still felt awkward in civilian clothes, after five years at war. Even a year of peace could not break him of the feeling he was out of uniform.

His hair was longer now, almost Bohemian enough to reach the collar of his best buttoned-up shirt. He looked every bit the young student in his tweed jacket as he crossed the street to reach the edge of the little park.

It had haunted him for years, this place. The train ride from Leningrad had made it seem more dreamlike as he approached, rather than less. Sergey thought of fairy mounds and elves.

He took a moment to center himself. Deep breaths.

Nazi tank regiments had not scared him this much.

A voice in his mind sent soothing tones. Tatiyana, dressed in her same, strange attire from the future, but somehow more formal. The bodysuit that showed her lean, spare frame, but with a bolero jacket over it and a sash. Perhaps she felt the same need to be dressed nicely. The future, after all, was about to find them again.

*You will do fine, dedushka. And I will be there to support you. I have wanted to meet her for a very long time.*

Sergey smiled in spite of himself, wondered just how much free will he really had anymore as he entered the park and looked around.

There.

A spot of blond hair. A girl, seated on a park bench, just as he had first seen her in his dreams, all those years ago. Pretty. Petite. Strong. A flowery sun dress over a demure white blouse.

For a moment, Sergey watched her read from a large book. Until now, he had known, but he had never truly *believed*.

He had dreamed about her, this lovely young woman, this Valeriya. He had named his first tank after her, years before he ever knew who she was. In his memory, he knew her voice, her smile, her lover's touch.

Right now, however, he stopped, tongue-tied and panicked. He felt Tatiyana's strong hand, but he could not take another step.

How would he explain to this stranger, this woman, that he had dreamed about her, held her, loved her? Even for a Russian fairy tale, it was insane.

Sergey stood there, bereft.

And then she looked up. Valeriya.

Brilliant blue eyes. A wisp of blond hair pulled loose by a breeze fluttered in her face.

Her eyes met his across the gap. And then a spark of recognition.

She smiled.

# About the Author

Blaze has lived in many different places, including Kansas, The Ozarks, Breckenridge, and SoCal. He's also done a number of things, some of which are even past the statute of limitations now. The ones he'll tell you about (without the need for full anonymity) include being a bouncer at a cowboy bar outside a Marine base, a volunteer storm-spotter with the county fire department, and herding nerds at a small software company. He currently lives Seattle-ish and tells stories in most every form of English you can, and a few other languages.

### Never miss a release!
If you'd like to be notified of new releases, sign up for my newsletter.

I only send out newsletters once a quarter, will never spam you, or use your email for nefarious purposes. You can also unsubscribe at any time.

http://www.blazeward.com/newsletter/

### Reviews
It's true. Reviews help me sell more books. If you've enjoyed this collection, please consider leaving a review of it on your favorite site.

# About Knotted Road Press

Knotted Road Press fiction specializes in dynamic writing set in mysterious, exotic locations.

Knotted Road Press non-fiction publishes autobiographies, business books, cookbooks, and how-to books with unique voices.

Knotted Road Press creates DRM-free ebooks as well as high-quality print books for readers around the world.

With authors in a variety of genres including literary, poetry, mystery, fantasy, and science fiction, Knotted Road Press has something for everyone.

Knotted Road Press
www.KnottedRoadPress.com

**Also available from Knotted Road Press**
**Beyond the Mirror: Volume 1 & 2**
**Fantastic Worlds**

Find them online at www.KnottedRoadPress.com or at your favorite bookseller